Breakout

BY RICHARD STARK

The Hunter [Payback]
The Man with the Getaway Face
The Outfit
The Mourner
The Score
The Jugger
The Seventh
The Handle
The Damsel
The Rare Coin Score
The Green Eagle Score
The Dame
The Black Ice Score
The Sour Lemon Score
Deadly Edge
The Blackbird
Slayground
Lemons Never Lie
Plunder Squad
Butcher's Moon
Comeback
Backflash
Flashfire
Firebreak

RICHARD STARK

Breakout

MYSTERIOUS PRESS™

Published by Warner Books

An AOL Time Warner Company

Copyright © 2002 by Richard Stark
All rights reserved.

 Mysterious Press books are published by Warner Books, Inc., 1271 Avenue of the Americas, New York, NY 10020.

Visit our Web site at www.twbookmark.com.
Visit www.donaldwestlake.com.

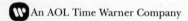 An AOL Time Warner Company

The Mysterious Press name and logo are registered trademarks of Warner Books, Inc.

Printed in the United States of America

First Printing: November 2002

10   9   8   7   6   5   4   3   2   1

Library of Congress Cataloging-in-Publication Data
Stark, Richard.
      Breakout / Richard Stark.
          p. cm.
      ISBN 0-89296-779-X
      1. Parker (Fictitious character)—Fiction.   2. Criminals—Fiction.
I. Title.

PS3573.E9 B74 2002
813'.54—dc21   2002023492

ONE

1

When the alarm went off, Parker and Armiston were far to the rear of the warehouse, Armiston with the clipboard, checking off the boxes they'd want. The white cartons were stacked six feet high to make aisles that stretched to the unpainted concrete block side walls of the building. A wider central aisle ran straight to the loading dock where they'd come in, dismantling the alarms and raising the overhead door.

Then what was *this* alarm, five minutes after they'd broken in? "That idiot Bruhl," Armiston said, throwing the clipboard away in exasperation. "He went into the office."

Parker was already loping toward the central aisle. Behind him, Armiston cried, "God *damn* it! Fingerprints!" and ran back to pick up the clipboard.

Parker turned into the main aisle, running, and

saw far away the big door still open, the empty truck backed against it. George Walheim, the lockman who'd got them in here, stood by the open doorway, making jerky movements, not quite running away.

These were all generic pharmaceuticals in here, and Armiston had the customer, at an airfield half an hour north. The plan was, by tomorrow these medicines would be offshore, more valuable than in the States, and the four who'd done the job would earn a nice percentage.

But that wasn't going to happen. Bruhl, brought in by Armiston, was supposed to have gotten a fork-lift truck, so he could run it down the main aisle to pick up the cartons Parker and Armiston had marked. Instead of which, he'd gone to see what he could lift from the office. But Walheim hadn't cleared the alarm system in the office.

As Parker ran down the long aisle, Armiston a dozen paces behind, Bruhl appeared, coming fast out of the first side aisle down there. Walheim tried to clutch at him, but Bruhl hit him with a backhand that knocked the thinner man down.

Parker yelled, "Bruhl! Stop!" but Bruhl kept going. He jumped to the ground outside the loading dock, next to the truck, then ran toward the front of it. He was going to take it, leave the rest of them here on foot.

There was no way to stop him, no way to get there in time. Walheim was still on hands and knees, looking for his glasses, when the truck jolted away from the loading dock. Outside was the darkness of four A.M., spotted with thin lights high on the corners of other buildings in this industrial park.

The truck, big rear doors flapping, heeled hard on the right turn at the end of the blacktop lot, Bruhl still accelerating. The empty truck was top-heavy, it wasn't going to make it.

Walheim was on his feet, patting his glasses into place, when Parker ran by. "What do we—?" But Parker was gone, jumping off the loading dock to run away leftward as behind him the truck crashed over onto its side and scraped along the pavement until it ran into a utility pole, knocking it over. The few lights around here went dark.

There was nothing in this area but the industrial park, empty at night. No houses, no bars, no churches, no schools. There were no pedestrians out here at four in the morning, no cars driving by.

Parker had run less than a block when he heard the sirens, far behind him but coming fast. There was nowhere to go to cover, no point trying to break into another of these buildings. Fleets of trucks here and there stood in lines behind high fences.

Parker kept running. Armiston and Walheim were wherever they wanted to be, and Parker tried to keep the sound of sirens behind him. But the sirens spread, left and right and then everywhere, slicing and dicing the night.

Parker ran down the middle of an empty street and ahead of him headlights came around a corner, a bright searchlight beam fastened on him. He stopped. He put his hands on top of his head.

2

Do you want to tell me about it?" the CID man offered.

"No," Parker said.

The CID man nodded, looking at him. He was small but bulky, a middleweight, carrot-topped, said his name was Turley. Inspector Turley. He had a dossier on the desk in front of him, Parker in the wooden chair opposite him, all of it watched by the two uniforms in the corners of this plain functional government-issue office. Turley opened the dossier and glanced at it with the air of a man who already knows what's inside, the grim satisfaction of somebody whose negative prediction has come true. "Ronald Kasper," he said, and frowned at Parker. "That isn't your name, is it?"

Parker watched him.

Turley looked down at the dossier again, rapped the middle knuckle of the middle finger of his right hand against the information in there. "That's the name on some fingerprints, belong to a fella escaped from a prison camp in California some years ago. Killed a guard on the way out." He raised an eyebrow at Parker. "You've got his fingerprints."

"The system makes mistakes," Parker said.

Turley's grin turned down, not finding anything funny here. "So do individuals, my friend," he said. Looking into his dossier again, he said, "There is no Ronald Kasper, not before, not since. In the prison camp, out, left behind these prints, one guard dead. Do you want to know *his* name?"

Parker shook his head. "Wouldn't mean anything to me."

"No, I suppose it wouldn't. We have some other names for you."

Parker waited. Turley raised an eyebrow at him, also waiting, but then saw that Parker had nothing to say and went back to the dossier. "Let me know which of these names you'd rather be. Edward Johnson. Charles Willis. Edward Lynch. No? Nothing? I have here a Parker, no first name. Still not?"

"Stick with Kasper," Parker said.

"Because we've got that one tied to your fingers any-way," Turley said, and leaned back. "We've got you all, you know. I imagine you'll be tried together." Turley didn't need his dossier now. "Armiston and Walheim are also in cells here," he said. "You probably won't see them until trial, but they're here. This is a big place."

It was. It was called Stoneveldt Detention Center, and it was where everybody charged with a state felony in this state spent their time before and during trial, unless they made bail, which Parker and Armiston and Walheim would not. No judge would look at their three histories and expect them to come back for their bail money.

Like the industrial park where things had gone wrong last night, Stoneveldt was on the outskirts of the only large city in this big empty midwestern state. Parker's few looks out windows since being brought here last night had shown him nothing out there but flat prairie, straight roads, a few more buildings of an industrial or governmental style, and a city rising far to the east. If he were still here for the trial, it would be a forty-minute bus ride in to court every morning and back out every night, looking at that prairie through iron mesh.

"Steven Bruhl," Turley went on, following his own train of thought, "is a little different. A local boy, to begin with."

Armiston had brought Bruhl in, needing somebody good with machinery like forklifts, not knowing he was an idiot. Well, they all knew it now. And Turley had said they *three* were all here in Stoneveldt, so where did that put Bruhl? Dead? Hospital?

"If Bruhl lives," Turley said, answering the question, "he'll be tried later on, after you three. So, unlike you, he'll already know what the future's gonna bring. And also unlike you, he won't have a chance to flip. Nobody left to rat on."

They sat there and watched that thought move around the room. The two uniforms shifted their feet, rubbed their backs against the wall, and watched Parker without expectation; he would not make them earn their pay or prove their training.

"Now, you," Turley said, "are in a better position. Out in front. You know game theory, Ronald?"

"Mr. Kasper," Parker said.

Turley snorted. "What difference does it make? That isn't your name anyway."

"You're right," Parker said, and spread his hands: Call me whatever you want.

"Game theory," Turley said, "suggests that whoever flips first wins, because there's nothing left for anybody else to sell."

"I've heard that," Parker agreed.

"Now, we've got you, and we've got the others," Turley said, "and you know as well as I do, we've got you cold. So what more do we want? What more could we possibly need, that we might want to bargain with you?"

"Not to walk," Parker said.

Turley seemed surprised. "Walk? Away from *this*? No, you know what we're talking about. Reduction in sentence, better choice of prison. Some of our prisons are better than others, you know."

"If you say so."

"Which means," Turley said, "though nobody will admit this, that some of our prisons must be worse. Maybe a *lot* worse." Turley leaned forward over the desk and the dossier, to impart a confidence. "We've got one hellhole," he said, his voice dropping, "and I wish we didn't, but there it is, where in that prison population you've only got three choices." He checked them off on his fingers. "White power, or black power, or dead."

"State should do something about that," Parker said.

"It's budget cuts," Turley told him. "The politicians, you know, they want everybody locked up, but they don't want to pay for it. So the prison administrators, they do what's called assignment of resources, meaning at least *some* of the facilities retain some hope of civilization." Turley leaned back. "One of you boys," he said, "is gonna wind up in a country club. The other two, it's a crapshoot."

Parker waited.

Turley looked at him, getting irritated at this lack of feedback. He said, "You probably wonder, if the state's already got *me*, what more can they want? What's my bargaining chip?"

Parker already knew. He already knew this entire conversation, but it was one of the steps he had to go through before he would be left alone to work things out for himself. He watched Turley, and waited.

Turley nodded, swiveling slightly in his chair. "Those drugs you boys were after," he said, "or medicines, I guess I should say, not to confuse the issue, where they'd really be worth your time and effort is overseas. But one of the reasons that distribution center was built in this area is because here we're in the middle of America, you can get anywhere in the country in no time at all from here. But not overseas. We're six hundred miles from an ocean or a border. Any ocean, any border. You boys were not gonna drive that truck six hundred miles. You had some other idea, and that other idea means there were more people involved. *That's* what you can trade us. Where were you taking the truck, who was going to be there, and what was the route after that?"

Turley waited, and so did Parker. Turley leaned forward again, forearm on the open dossier on the desk. "No?"

"I'll think about it," Parker said.

"Meaning you won't, not so far," Turley told him. "But what about Armiston? What about Walheim? What about Bruhl, when he comes to?"

"If," Parker said, because he wanted to know how bad Bruhl was.

Bad, because Turley nodded and shrugged and said, "All right, if. But he still could come through, he's a young strong guy. The point is, *you*. You know these friends of yours, Armiston and Walheim. Is one of them gonna make the jump before you?"

"We'll see," Parker said.

Turley stood, ending the session. The uniforms

stood straighter, away from the walls. Parker looked around, then also stood.

"Think about it," Turley said. "If you want to talk to me, any time at all, tell the guard."

"Right," Parker said.

3

It isn't just this cell," Williams said. "The whole place is overcrowded."

Parker could believe it. The cell he was in, with Williams and two others, here on the third tier of a four-tier cage built inside an outer shell of concrete block, was eight feet by six, meant to house two short-term prisoners, but double-decker bunks had been put in to crowd four men into the space, and the court dockets were also crowded, so much so that inmates weren't here for the month or two the architects had counted on but for eight months, ten months, a year.

This was a strange place because it was a prison and yet it wasn't a prison. There was no stable population, no long-termers to keep it cohesive. Everybody was transient, even though the transit was longer and more uncomfortable than it was supposed to be.

This was the place before the decisions were made, so this was the place of hope. There was always that chance; a witness would disappear, the lab would screw up, the court would buy your lawyer's argument. When this transient period was done, when your time in court was finished, you'd leave here, either for the street or to go deeper into the system, into a penitentiary, and until the last second of the last day of your trial you could never be absolutely sure which way it would go.

But because it was a place of hope, of possibilities, of decisions not yet made, it was also a place of paranoia. You didn't know any of these guys. You were all strangers to one another, not here long enough to have developed a reputation, not going to stay long enough to want to form into groups. The only thing you knew for sure was that there *were* rats in the pop, people ready to pass on to the law anything they might learn about you, either because they'd been put here specifically for that purpose, or because they were opportunists, ready to market in pieces of information because it might put them in good with the authorities; push themselves up by pushing you down. And it would probably work, too.

So people didn't talk in here, not about anything that mattered, not about what they'd done or who they were or what they thought their prospects might be. They'd bitch about their court-appointed lawyers or about the food, they'd talk religion if they were that kind, or sports, but they'd never let anybody else put a handle on their back.

The one good thing about all this isolation was that no gangs formed, no race riots happened. The Aryan Nations guys with their swastika tattoos and the Black Power guys with their monks' hoods could glower and mutter at one another, but they couldn't make a crew, because anybody could be a rat, anybody, even if he looked just like you.

In the cell with Parker were one black guy, Williams, plus an Hispanic and a white, Miscellaneous, neither of whom volunteered their names or anything else when Parker arrived and flipped open the mattress on the top bunk, right. Williams, a big guy, medium brown, with a genial smile and reddened eyes, was a natural talker, so even in here he'd say *something*; introducing himself when Parker was first led in: "Williams."

"Kasper," Parker told him, because that's the name the law was using.

Neither of them had much more to say at that point, and the other two, both short scrawny guys with permanent vertical frown lines in their foreheads, said nothing and avoided eye contact. But later that day, their section got library time, and those two trooped off with perhaps half the tier to the library.

"Working on their cases," Williams said, with a grin.

"Law library in there?"

"They aren't readers."

"They aren't lawyers, either," Parker said.

Williams grinned again. "They're dumbfuck

peons," he said. "Like you and me. But it keeps them calm. They're working on their cases."

Yes, it was the dumbfuck peons who'd gone off to work on their cases, but Parker could tell the difference between them and Williams. The whole pop in here was in white T-shirt and blue jeans and their own shoes, so it shouldn't have been possible to say anything about people's backgrounds or education or anything else just from looking at them, but you could tell. The ones who went off to work on their cases wore their clothes dirty and wrinkled and sagging; their jaws jutted but their shoulders slumped. Looking up and down the line, you could see the ones who were brighter, more sure of themselves. You still couldn't tell from looking at a guy if he was square or a fink, but you could make an accurate class judgment in the snap of a finger.

Parker would usually be as silent in here as the other two, but he wanted to know about this place, and the sooner the better. Williams, an educated guy—no telling what he, or anybody else, was in here for—clearly liked to take an interest in his surroundings. And he also liked to talk, about the overcrowding or anything else that wasn't personal.

Parker said, "A couple others came in with me. I'm wondering how to get in touch with them."

Williams shook his head. "Never happen," he said. "I come in with another fella myself. I understand he's up on four, heard that from my lawyer."

Parker hadn't been reached by a lawyer yet; that was the next necessity. He said, "So my partners are gonna be on different floors."

"It's a big joint," Williams said, "and they do that on purpose. They don't want you and your pals working out your story together, ironing out the little kinks. Keep you separate." Williams' grin was mocking but sad; knowing the story but stuck in it anyway. "They can go to your pal," he said, "tell him, Kasper's talking. Come to you, say, your pal's talking."

Parker nodded. They had the cell doors open this time of day, so he stepped out and leaned on the iron bar of the railing there, overlooking the drop to the concrete floor outside the cage. Heavy open mesh screen was fixed along the face of the cage, top to bottom, to keep people from killing themselves.

Parker stood there awhile, watching guards and prisoners move around down below, and then he went back in and climbed up to sit on his bunk. Williams was in the lower across the way. He looked up at Parker and said, "You're thinking hard."

"I've got to," Parker said.

4

The second day, the loudspeaker said, "Kasper," and when Parker walked down the aisle past the cages in the cage to the gated stairwell at the end, the guard at the metal desk there said, "Kasper?"

"Yes."

There was another guard present, standing by the stairs. He said, "Lawyer visit."

The first guard pressed the button on his desk, the buzzer sounded, and the second guard pulled open the door. Parker went through and down the stairs, the second guard following. The stairs were metal, patterned with small circular holes, and loud when you walked on them.

At the bottom, Parker and the guard turned right and went through a locked barred door into a short broad windowless corridor painted pale yellow, with a black composition floor. A white line was painted down the middle of the floor and everybody walked to

the right. There was a fairly steady stream of foot traffic in the corridor, because this was the only way in to
the cells; prisoners, guards, clerks, a minister, a doctor.

One more guard seated at a table beside one more
barred door to be unlocked, and they could go
through into the front part of the building, with an ordinary broad corridor down the middle of it, people
walking however they wanted. The doorways from this
corridor had no doors. The wide opening on the right
led to the mess hall, which took up all the space on
that side. The first doorway on the left was the library,
with the inmates in there lined up in front of the electric typewriters, waiting their ten-minute turn to work
on their case. The doorway at the far end led to the
visitors' room, and the doorway halfway along on the
left was for lawyer visits.

"In there," the guard said, and Parker went through
into a broad room with a wide table built into it that
stretched wall-to-wall from left to right. At four-foot in-
tervals, plywood partitions rose from the table to head-
height, to create privacy areas. Chairs on this side faced
the table between the partitions, numbered on their
backs. Three of the chairs were occupied by inmates,
talking to people across the table, lawyers presumably,
blocked from Parker's sight by the partitions. "Number
three," the guard said, and Parker went over to chair
number three. In the chair on the other side, facing
him, was a black man in a brown suit, pale blue shirt,
yellow tie, all of it wrinkled. He wore gold-framed

glasses and his hair was cropped short. He was looking in the briefcase open on the table, but then looked over at Parker and said, "Good morning, Ronald."

"Good morning." Parker sat facing him and put his forearms on the table.

"I'm Jacob Sherman," the man said, "I'll be your attorney."

"You got a card?" Parker asked him.

Surprised, Sherman said, "Of course," and reached into his suit-coat pocket. The card he handed Parker showed he was alone, not with a firm. Parker looked at it and put it away.

Sherman said, "I wish I had good news for you."

"I don't expect good news," Parker said.

"George Walheim," Sherman said, and paused, then, seeming embarrassed, said, "had a heart attack. He's in the hospital."

A heart attack. Walheim hadn't expected things to go wrong. Parker said, "So that's two of us in the hospital. Is Bruhl still alive?"

"Oh, yes," Sherman said. "He'll be all right, eventually."

"Is Armiston in here?"

"I really wouldn't know," Sherman said. "He's being represented by someone else."

So that string was gone. The four down to two, the two separated. Parker didn't think he could work this next part single-o, but how do you build a string in a place like this? He said, "How long, do you think, before trial?"

"Oh, I don't think that's going to happen," Sherman said.

Parker said, "You don't think a *trial* is gonna happen?"

"Well, California is certainly going to request extradition," Sherman told him.

"No," Parker said. "We fight that."

Sherman seemed surprised. "Why bother? You'll have to go there sooner or later."

Any other environment they put him in would be worse than this, harder to handle. Particularly if he was in a jurisdiction where he was known as someone who had both escaped and killed a guard. He said, "I'd rather deal with the local issue first."

"California," Sherman said, "will argue that their murder charge takes precedence."

"But I'm *here*," Parker said. "That should take precedence. We can argue it."

It was clear that Sherman didn't want the work involved; it was too pleasant to think of this case as a simple one, a fellow here today, on his way to California tomorrow. "I'll see what I can do," he said.

"You can do something else for me," Parker said.

"Yes?"

"There's a woman doesn't know what's happened to me. She'll worry. I don't want to phone her from here, or write her through the censors, because I don't want her connected to me, don't want to make trouble for her." He pointed at the briefcase. "You'll have some paper in there, and an envelope. I want to write her, so she'll know I'm still alive, and put it in the envelope, and address it. I'll ask you to put the stamp on it and mail it, and not show it to the people here. I won't ask her to do anything illegal, this is just so she won't worry, but I won't get the law complicating her life."

Sherman looked away, toward the guards at the doors, the prisoners' door and the lawyers' door. Then he looked at Parker and nodded. "I can do that."

"Thank you."

What Sherman gave him was a yellow lined sheet of paper from a long legal pad, and a pen, and an envelope with Sherman's office address on it for the return. Parker wrote, "This place is called Stoneveldt. I'm here as Ronald Kasper. Get me a mouth I can use." No heading and no signature. He folded the paper, put it in the envelope, sealed it, wrote "Claire Willis, East Shore Rd., Colliver's Pond, NJ 08989" on the front, then said, "You got Scotch tape in there?"

"I think so."

Sherman rooted around in the briefcase, came up with a roll of tape, handed it over. Parker taped the flap, then folded a length of tape along all four edges. Now it couldn't be opened without leaving traces. He pushed the envelope and the roll of tape over to Sherman, saying, "I appreciate it. I've been worried about her."

Sherman looked at the envelope. "New Jersey. Long way from here."

"Yes."

"You'd have been better off staying there."

"I didn't know that then," Parker said.

"No." Sherman tapped the return address on the envelope. "If your friend has questions, she can get in touch with me."

"She probably will."

Putting letter and tape away, Sherman said, "We haven't talked about the arraignment. I assume you want to plead not guilty."

"Sure. When is it?"

"It's scheduled now for a week from Thursday."

Parker frowned at him. "That long? For an arraignment?"

"The courts are really quite clogged," Sherman told him. "But it doesn't matter that much, whatever time you do in here counts on your sentence."

"Yeah, there's that," Parker said. "And it gives us more time to argue the extradition thing. They can't start that until after the arraignment."

"We'll do what we can," Sherman said. "Do you have any other questions? Anything else I should do? People to contact?"

"No, if you just send that to Claire so she knows I'm alive, then I won't worry about things."

"Good." Sherman stuck his hand out. "Nice to chat with you, Ronald."

"Thank you, Mr. Sherman."

They both stood, and Sherman said, "See you at the arraignment."

"Right," Parker said, knowing he'd never see Mr. Sherman again.

5

The first week is the hardest. The change from outside, from freedom to confinement, from spreading your arms wide to holding them in close to your body, is so abrupt and extreme that the mind refuses to believe it. Second by second, it keeps on being a rotten surprise, the worst joke in the world. You keep thinking, I can't stand this, I'm going to lose my mind, I'm going to wig out or off myself, I can't stand this *now* and *now* and *now.*

Then, sometime in the second week, the mind's defenses kick in, the brain just flips over, and this place, this impossible miserable place, just becomes the place where you happen to live. These people are the people you live among, these rules are the rules you live within. This is your world now, and it's the other one that isn't real any more.

Parker wondered if he'd be here that long.

The stolid regularity of the routine helped in this process of turning the inmate into a con. In Stoneveldt, the day began at six, when the cell gates were electrically rolled open, loudly, but then nothing happened until seven-twenty, when everyone on three was to line up by the door to the stairs. It was opened, and in single file they thudded down the flights and through the corridor with the white line on the floor into the main building and on into the mess hall there. They arrived at seven-thirty and had to be out by seven fifty-five. The inmates on four had breakfast there at seven, those from two at eight, and those on the ground floor at eight-thirty.

After breakfast they were trooped back up to their floor, but the cell gates were left open, and there was a game room with playing cards and board games and a television set down at the opposite end from the stairs. This was the time when those who felt sick could be escorted to the dispensary.

At ten-thirty they were led downstairs again, but this time down the long concrete floor between the outer wall and the ground floor cells to iron doors at the rear that opened onto the exercise yard. Armiston wasn't on the ground floor, those cells being given to the nondangerous sad sacks, the drunk drivers, domestic disputes, deadbeat dads. The exercise yard, enclosed by high unpainted concrete block walls, was packed dirt, with a weight-lifting area and one basketball hoop.

Three's lunch period was twelve forty-five to one-thirty, and afternoon outside time three-thirty to four-thirty. Also in the afternoon was the time when the prisoners could go off to the library to find something to read or to work on their case.

Morning and afternoon, after breakfast and after lunch, a group of names was called on the loud-speaker, and those cons went off on assignments. The way it was structured, everybody was given work to do, a half day three times a week, in the kitchen or the laundry or paint detail or mopping the floors. Skilled men fixed toilets and television sets. During those times, Parker found people to talk with, get a sense of, remember for later.

Dinner six-thirty to seven-thirty. At nine, everybody had to be back in his cage. The cell gates rolled shut. The lights went out.

6

The fifth day, the loudspeaker said, "Kasper," and the guard said, "Lawyer visit," but it wasn't wrinkled Jacob Sherman, looking to duck the work of fighting extradition. It was an older man, Asian, hair sleeked back and flesh gleaming, who rose in Armani and pastels on his side of the table. "I am Mr. Li," he said, and extended a card without being asked.

The card was full of names and addresses, all in blue print on ivory, with "Jonathan Li" in gold on the bottom right. Parker put it away and said, "You've got me now."

"Transfer complete." Li was amused, not by Parker in particular but by his own entire life; it made him easy to be around, but suggested there were circumstances when he might not be completely reliable. "We should sit," he said. "For the quiet."

They sat, and Parker waited, watching him. His smoothly sheathed forearms on the tabletop, wrists delicately crossed, Li leaned a bit forward as he talked, to keep the conversation within their space. "Your friend Claire wants me to assure you she's fine."

"Good."

"And that she expects to see you soon."

"We can only hope," Parker said.

"Oh, we can do more than hope," Li told him.

"I understand California wants me," Parker said.

"California must wait its turn."

"That's what I thought."

"Oh, yes," Li said. "My professional opinion is, you should not leave this place until you want to leave this place."

"That's good," Parker said.

"Also, as you may know," Li went on, "if you are to have any visitor other than immediate members of your family, you must put in the request yourself, from this end, and the authorities will or will not approve of it. Unfortunately, you have no immediate family nearby—"

"No."

"—but it happens that your former brother-in-law is working on a construction job not terribly far from here and would be happy to have that opportunity to visit you while you're in confinement."

"My former brother-in-law," Parker said.

"I believe at one time he was married to your sister Debby."

Parker had no sister Debby. He said, "Oh, sure."

"So your former brother-in-law, Ed Mackey—"

"Ah," Parker said. That was more real than sister Debby.

Li smiled at him. "Yes, I thought you'd be pleased."

"Even surprised," Parker said.

"As I understand it," Li said, "you and your brother-in-law have been partners in business enterprises in the past, and he believes you might be interested in a similar business enterprise once your current legal problems have been resolved."

"He's probably right about that," Parker said.

Li also had a briefcase, like Sherman, but his was on the floor and was much more glossy and polished. Dipping into it, Li came out with a thin sheaf of forms. "This is the application," he said. "I've filled in Mr. Mackey's part."

Parker took the form. He hadn't expected anybody else to take a hand in this. "I'm looking forward to seeing Ed," he said, meaning it, then looked at Li: "I understand the arraignment's next Thursday."

"Oh, I don't think we'll be ready by then," Li said. He seemed comfortable with the idea.

Parker said, "We'll delay it?"

Li unfolded his wrists to open expressive hands, like lily pads opening. "You are, after all, the client," he said. "I believe you're in no hurry to alter your situation, in regard to these charges and so on. Am I right?"

"You're right."

"I thought so." Rising, putting out a hand to shake,

he said, "I won't take up any more of your time unless I have news."

Shaking that firm hand, Parker said, "There won't be news for a while."

"Only your brother-in-law."

Parker grinned. "I'm looking forward to that."

7

It looks to me," Ed Mackey said, "as though you zigged when you should have zagged."

"There was a local hand," Parker said, "dumber than he had to be."

Mackey nodded. "I read about it in the local papers."

This was a different place from where he'd met with the lawyers, farther along the same corridor in the same building, a more open place like a cafeteria, with bare metal tables and metal chairs, and soda and snack vending machines in a row on one wall. There were family groups and single visitors, with a steady surf sound of conversation, guards walking around but nobody standing over you.

The rules in here were few and simple. The prisoners were not to put their hands under the table, and no object of any kind, not even an Oreo cookie, was to pass between a prisoner and any visitor, not even an infant. To break either rule was to be removed from the visitor room immediately and strip-searched; and probably to lose visitation rights, at least for a while

When Parker had been led in here, Mackey was already seated at a small square table away from the vending machines and the loudest family groups. Mackey, stocky, blunt-featured, and blunt-bodied, didn't rise but grinned and waved a greeting. Parker went over and sat with him, and when Mackey said he'd been reading the local papers, he asked, "You reading up on more than one thing?"

"Not around here."

"Good." Parker frowned at him. "I didn't know you'd be in this part of the world."

Mackey laughed. "I didn't know *you'd* be here either," he said. "You wanna know why I'm here?"

"Yes."

"There was a fella we used to know named George Liss."

"That's right."

"And because you were there, too," Mackey said, "I'm still alive." What he didn't add, not in a place like this, was that Liss was not still alive, and Parker'd done that, too.

So Mackey felt he owed Parker one, because in truth Liss had tried to kill them both, and in saving himself Parker had saved Mackey as well. Parker didn't keep scorecards like that, but he didn't mind if Mackey wanted to. He said, "I appreciate it."

"*De nada,*" Mackey said. "Anything I can do to make life a little brighter?"

"One thing now."

"Sure."

"This is all transient," Parker told him. "The whole population, everybody moving through. Tough to get a read on anybody."

"You need histories," Mackey suggested.

"And if it's somebody I can talk to," Parker said, "then I need a friend of his on the outside to tell him I'm all right."

Mackey wore a zippered jacket, and now he took from its inner pocket a memo pad and pen, which attracted the attention of a guard. The guard watched, but Parker kept his hands flat on the table and Mackey leaned back, pad on the palm of his left hand. "Go," he said.

"Brandon Williams. Bob Clayton. Walter Jelinek. Tom Marcantoni."

Putting the pad and pen away, Mackey said, "This is tricky. Very roundabout."

"All I got is time," Parker said.

That was the seventh day. Two days later, Mackey was back, looking pleased. "Brenda says hello," he said. Brenda was his lady, had been for a long time.

Parker said, "She with you?"

"Always," Mackey said. "She's never far away. She's somebody else saved my life once."

"You must be a bad risk," Parker said.

Mackey grinned. "Not if I keep hanging out with the right people."

Some years ago, Brenda had trailed Mackey and Parker, though she hadn't been asked to, when they went to deliver some stolen paintings in a deal that then went very bad. At the end, Parker left a lumberyard's burning main building, with the paintings destroyed, and he'd believed Mackey was dead, shot by one of the people who'd been waiting in there. Brenda, seeing Parker take off alone, went into the building, found Mackey on the concrete floor, and dragged him out and into her car before the fire engines arrived.

"Fortunately," Mackey said, "life is usually quieter than that."

"We like it quiet," Parker said.

"We do. Williams and Marcantoni might be good to talk to. They're both facing hard time like you, both got stand-up histories."

"Not the other two?"

"Clayton's in on a Mickey Mouse," Mackey said, "do a nickel tops. He doesn't need alternatives. And Jelinek's ratted people out before."

"Then we don't talk to Jelinek," Parker said.

8

There was the day Parker went on sick call, and the day he went to the library to work on his case, and the afternoons he spent on work detail in the kitchen, a long windowless bright-lit space in the basement under the mess hall, with siren-alarmed iron doors at one end where supplies were delivered.

The eleventh day, after the other two from the cell went off to work on their case, Williams got up from his bunk and tossed away his magazine and came out to where Parker leaned on the railing to watch the movement down below. Williams said, "I hear you know Chili Greebs."

Parker shook his head. "Never heard of him."

Surprised, Williams turned away to see what Parker was looking at down there. Watching the guards as they shifted their charges around, he said, "Then why should Chili tell me to talk to you?"

"Probably," Parker said, "it was after he talked with a friend of mine."

"Would he be a friend of mine?"

"Not yet. His name's Ed Mackey."

Williams grinned. Now that the tension was gone, you could see where it had been. He said, "That's the name I heard."

Parker said, "Ed told me you're all right, and he'd find somebody to tell you the same about me."

"Now we know and love each other," Williams said, "what next?"

"You're facing twenty-five to life," Parker told him.

Williams turned his head to look at Parker's profile. "Your friend Ed got this on the outside."

"Nobody gets anything in here."

Williams shrugged. "And so what?"

Parker said, "I'm not good at prison."

Williams laughed. "Who is?"

"Some are," Parker said.

Williams sobered, looking away again at the scene below. "And that's true," he said. He sounded as though he didn't like the thought.

"I don't think you are," Parker said.

Williams shook his head. "I can feel myself gettin smaller every day. You fight it, but there it is." He turned his head to study Parker's face. "You aren't thinking about breaking out of *here*."

"Why not?"

"This is not an easy place," Williams said.

"Better than some," Parker told him. "It's transient, it wasn't built to house this big a population, or for people to stay this long. The system's strained, and when I look around, they're short some guards. A state pen could be tougher, and you've already been beaten down for a few months."

"Jesus." Williams looked off. Beyond the mesh fence, out over the air, the concrete block wall featured long lines of plate-glass windows that bore no relationship to the levels of the floors inside the cage. "I've been setting it aside," he said. "Thinking I'd wait till I was in a stable place, where I could be part of a crew. I bet a lot of guys figure that way."

"I need the crew *here*," Parker said. "That's why I asked Ed Mackey to look around, find me somebody wasn't going to rat me out."

Williams shook his head. "Two guys? Is that enough?"

"I have a line on one more. Three should do it."

"Depends what we do. Who's this other one?"

"Do you know Tom Marcantoni?"

"Sounds white."

"He is."

"Then I wouldn't know him," Williams said. "I know you because we got a stateroom together."

"When you see me talk to somebody," Parker said, "that'll be Marcantoni."

Williams laughed. "You *don't* do a lot of talking, do you?"

"Only when I have to," Parker said.

9

Tom Marcantoni said, "Let's play a game of checkers." It was the first time he'd spoken to Parker, who had walked into the game room a while after his conversation with Brandon Williams. So Ed Mackey had been busy.

"Fine," Parker said.

The tables and chairs in the game room were metal, bolted to the floor. Marcantoni got a checkerboard and an open cardboard box of men from a shelf on the back wall while Parker found an empty table and sat at it. Marcantoni came over to join him and they started to play.

Parker waited, but for a while Marcantoni had nothing to say. He was a big man with a bullet head and a thick black single eyebrow that made him always look pissed off about something. Now he looked pissed off at the checkerboard and had nothing to say until he yawned hugely in the middle of a move, covering his mouth with the back of the hand holding the checker. Yawn done, he blinked at the board and said, "Shit. Where'd I get this thing from?"

Parker pointed at the square, and Marcantoni finished his move, then said, "I can't sleep in a place like this."

"I know," Parker said.

"It keeps me awake, this place, like a weight on my chest," Marcantoni said. He frowned at the board, didn't look directly at Parker. He said, "Any time I'm in a place like this, when I get out, the first thing I do, I sleep for a week. It isn't a natural environment, this."

"It isn't an environment," Parker said. "It's a body cast."

Now Marcantoni did look at Parker, peering at him from under that eyebrow as though looking out at a field from the edge of the woods. "You got *that* right," he said, then looked down at the board. "Whose move is it?"

"Mine," Parker said, and moved.

Marcantoni said, "A friend of mine says I should talk to you."

"Uh-huh."

"Do you know why?"

"Maybe," Parker said, "we could figure out a way to get a night's sleep."

Marcantoni nodded, and jumped one of Parker's pieces. "This game's too easy," he said. "Not like some games."

"The harder games take more concentration," Parker said.

"And more risk," Marcantoni said.

Parker said, "You're facing life. Not much risk left for you."

Marcantoni sat back, ignoring the board. "You know things about me," he said. "But I don't know diddly about you."

"Ask your friend."

"I will. You're thinking about a game for two?"

"Three," Parker said. "It wouldn't be a polite game. More a power game."

Marcantoni looked around at the other inmates in the room, playing their games, reading their magazines. "A lot of mutts around here," he said.

"There are," Parker agreed.

"You can't be too careful." Marcantoni nodded, agreeing with himself. "That's why you had your friend check me out and then go talk to my friend."

"That's right."

"So you've got a third guy?"

"One of my cellmates. Williams."

Marcantoni frowned, trying to place that, then said, "He's a black guy."

"Right."

Marcantoni made a sour face and shook his head. "You wanna work with a black guy?"

"Why not?"

"Group loyalty," Marcantoni said. "One of the first

things I learned in life, stick with the group where there's a chance for loyalty. There's never a guarantee, but a chance. A black guy doesn't feel loyalty for you and me. He'd trade us for chewing gum, and we'd do the same for him."

Parker said, "I've been here eleven days. I got the population on this floor to work with. Like you say, a lot of it's mutts. Some of it, all they're facing's a nickel-dime, it's not worth it to them, try a different game. From the rest, only two have a reputation I can take a chance on. You, and Williams. He isn't afraid to stand with you, so if you're afraid to stand with him I'll just have to look around, try to find somebody else."

"Instead of me, you mean," Marcantoni said.

Parker waited, looking at the board.

Marcantoni sighed, then yawned again, then laughed at himself. "I'm groggy, is what it is," he said. "Okay, fuck it, a new experience. Get outa your neighborhood, meet new friends."

"Good," Parker said.

"King me," Marcantoni said.

10

Because of the black-white thing, it was hard for them to meet, make a plan. If a black guy and a white guy who weren't cellmates talked to each other, people would want to know why. The guards would want to know, and some of the inmates would want to know. What have those guys got to talk to each other about? What's going on?

The answer was to work out with the weights. Only Marcantoni had been doing that before, but now Parker and Williams went over there, too, and could be in a little separate group without snagging anybody's interest.

The first thing Marcantoni and Williams had to do was get a sense of each other. Lifting hand weights in alternate moves, like walking up the air, not looking at anybody in particular, Marcantoni said, "I never had to rely on anybody your tone before."

"Same here," Williams said. Seated on a wooden

bench, weights strapped to his shins, he was lifting and lowering both feet together, from the knee.

"Maybe we got something we can share," Marcantoni said. "You got a religion?" Then he laughed at himself, lost his rhythm with the hand weights, found it again, and said, "Never mind, you were brought up Baptist, I don't even wanna know about it."

"And you're a fish-eater," Williams said. "I could tell from your nose."

"We don't do that any more," Marcantoni said.

Parker pressed a weighted bar up to his chest. "You don't have to like each other," he said.

Williams stood and jogged in place, the weights still on his shins. "But we have to trust each other," he said.

Marcantoni said, "How come you trust Kasper, that's what I don't get. He's a white guy."

"He looks like a door to me," Williams said. "I never did care what color a door was."

Parker lowered the bar, lifted it again. "We ready to talk?"

"Let's do it," Marcantoni said.

Williams said, "The only way out is through the front building."

"Well, you're right about that," Marcantoni told him. "This place's only got two exits. The back comes here, and we don't get through or over or under those walls, and the front goes to the front building, with all the ways out."

Parker said, "We can forget the kitchen. It's under

the mess hall and the only way out from there is kept solid locked, unless they're bringing supplies in or garbage out."

"Some places," Marcantoni said, "some guys got out in garbage cans. A little messy, but there you are, out."

"Here they know about that," Parker said. "They use plastic bags, and they back the compactor truck into the door opening, toss in the bags, compress them right there, before they go."

"Squish," said Williams.

Marcantoni grinned at him. "That was funny," he told him. "What you said."

Williams grinned back. "You think so?"

Parker said, "The dispensary is in the prison building, down by the foot of the stairs, before any doors at all, so there's no point doing sick call."

Williams said, "The laundry's in the basement, across the way from the kitchen. Just as impossible."

Marcantoni said, "If that leaves nothing but the visitors' room and the lawyers' room, I don't see us doing it without a tank."

Parker said, "There's the library."

Marcantoni put the hand weights on the shelf, stood contemplating the other possibilities lined up there. He said, "What does the library do for us?"

Parker said, "When you first go into the front building, there's the mess hall on the right, and the first thing on the left is the library."

"Sure," Marcantoni said.

"But it isn't the first thing," Parker told him. "Before that, at the very start of that wall on the left, there's another door."

"Closed and locked," Marcantoni said, and Williams, taking off his shin weights, said, "I've never seen anybody use it."

Parker said, "It's the way the guards come to work, a hall there next to the library, goes back to the offices. I *think* the way it works, the volunteer lawyer in the library, back in the stacks there where we're not allowed to go—"

"That's right," Williams said. "You tell the lawyer what you're looking for, he goes back and gets it, and you sign out for it."

"Back there," Parker said, "I *think* he's got a door to the guards' hall, a side door. He doesn't come around to the main corridor when he comes to work."

Marcantoni, sounding surprised that he remembered this detail, said, "He doesn't come outa there at all. When the library closes, he locks the door from the inside, stays in there."

"Goes out the back," Williams said.

Parker said, "We should all talk to our friends on the outside, get what floor plans we can't see for ourselves."

"And a car and driver waiting when we come out," Marcantoni said. "I don't wanna be calling a cab."

"When we get a route," Parker said, "we'll get a car."

"Good," Marcantoni said. "There's one thing more.

I was working on a better thing when I was nabbed on this thing. Half my crew came in with me, they're lost to me now. The rest will help us get out. But I'm gonna need cash, so I've gotta do this other thing, right away. I want you two in with me."

"Replacements," Williams said.

Parker didn't like where this was going. He said, "Is this something near here?"

"In the city, yeah."

"It's not smart," Parker told him, "to break out of here, then hang around the neighborhood, pull a job."

"It goes down easy," Marcantoni promised. "And I can keep you both out of sight, for just a few days. Then you're off wherever you go, with cash in your pocket."

Parker considered. He couldn't expect Marcantoni to describe the job to him, inside here, but it wasn't good to make a jump into the unknown. Still, he needed Marcantoni. So he'd go along with it, and if it looked bad, he could make adjustments.

Marcantoni said, "I'm trusting you in here. I'm asking you to trust me out there."

Parker nodded. "I'm in," he said.

"Me, too," Williams said. "Why not?"

Marcantoni said, "Good. You're gonna like it." He grinned at Williams. "You're okay for a Baptist," he said.

11

Ed Mackey said, "Marcantoni's friend was in on the armored car with him. Every day Marcantoni keeps his mouth shut, his friend owes him his life."

Parker said, "Does that make him grateful, or scared?"

"Grateful," Mackey said. "They did some things together, like you and me, they trust each other, he'd like his pal outside, be a help here and there."

"Sometimes," Parker said, "a guy wants to help somebody get to the outside, it turns out, he just wanted a clear shot on him."

"Not Marcantoni."

"Meaning what about Williams?"

Mackey shrugged and shook his head. "There it's family," he said. "So that's a little different, harder to read. Who I'm talking to is a neighbor of Williams' sister, a guy in a different line of business entirely."

"What line of business?"

"Import-export," Mackey said, and touched the tip of his nose. "You know what I mean."

"Mostly import?"

"I'd say so, yeah."

"Trade?"

"No, he sells to the trade." Mackey grinned. "You seen those signs on the stores. 'To the trade only.' Wholesalers. He's like that."

"But Williams isn't part of it."

"No, Williams is strictly a heavy, like you or me. He doesn't deal in anything and he doesn't taste anything."

"And his sister?"

"A simple girl, I think an innocent. Loves her brother."

"I hate not being able to see these people," Parker said. "Is there any way she can shop me and not shop her brother?"

"Not that I can see," Mackey said, and offered a slow smile. "And at this point," he said, "she and the neighbor are a little afraid of me."

Parker looked at him. "Just a little?"

"So far," Mackey said.

That was the twelfth day. The thirteenth, Mackey gave him a verbal map. "From what I hear," he said, "that doorway you use, when you come in here, that's a corridor straight down from the cells, mess hall on the right, the other side of that wall there with the kids' pictures of trees and airplanes and shit."

"I visit the lawyers across the same corridor," Parker told him, "beyond that wall with the long table and the drinking fountain."

"Right," Mackey said. "And from what I understand, the library's beyond that, the hallway you want beyond that."

"Right."

"Okay, tilt it all on its side," Mackey told him, because they wouldn't be able to write any of this down or make any drawings. "You know those metal change things the conductors carry on the front of their belt, where they can give you coins out of?"

"Right."

"Okay. Then if this whole thing is on its side with that corridor out there on the bottom, then where we are is the row of half dollars, and the lawyers' room next to it is the row of quarters, and the library is the row of dimes, and the hallway you want to know about is the row of nickels. Okay?"

"Right," Parker said.

"Near the top of the dimes, the library," Mackey said, "back where the law books are kept, there's a side door to the hallway, the row of nickels."

"That's what I hoped."

"It's kept locked, and the lawyer doesn't have the key. In fact, there is no key. When he wants out, he phones, and the guard at the far end of the hallway, top of the nickels, buzzes him out. Same going in, buzzes him in."

"What's beyond the guard at the far end of the hallway?"

"Above the nickels and the dimes is a couple of-fices and the guards' locker room, where they change for work. And a side door to the guards' separate parking lot."

"Good. What else?"

"Above the lawyers, and you see the corner of this room where the door is that I come in, above all that is the hall down from the front entrance at the very top of the building. The rest up there is offices and johns."

"So the best route out," Parker said, "looks as though it's into the library, into that side hallway, in the guards' locker room, into the guards' parking area. Is the parking area kept guarded and locked?"

"You know it is."

"So I need," Parker said, "people coming in while I'm coming out."

"I can talk to Marcantoni's pal," Mackey said.

"And Williams' sister, and her friend?"

"I don't think I'll mention many details to them," Mackey said.

12

Walter Jelinek was a man, but he looked like a car, the kind of old junker car that had been in some bad accidents so that now the frame is bent, the wheels don't line up any more, the whole vehicle sags to one side and pulls to that side, and the brakes are oatmeal. Half the original body is gone, the paint job is some amateur brushwork, and there's duct tape over the taillights. That was Walter Jelinek, who Mackey had told Parker not to talk to, since he had a reputation for carrying tales to teacher, but now Jelinek on his own wanted to talk to Parker.

It was the fourteenth day, two weeks in this hard world, progress but slow, and Parker was on his way to join Marcantoni and Williams over by the weights in the exercise yard when all at once Jelinek was beside him, gimping along with him, trying to keep in step. His left shoulder was low, his left knee had a ding in it that made it click outward when he walked, and his jaw hadn't been rewired very well, so that he always showed some spaces and some teeth. His hands were big but bunchy, and when he talked he sounded as though something was knotted too tight around his neck. He said, "Kasper, you and me, we never talk somehow."

Parker stopped, to look at him. Guards always kept their eyes on Jelinek, because he was like a garden to them, something always ripening. Aware that guards now watched him talk to Jelinek, Parker said, "We never talk because we got nothing to say to one another."

"Couple old lags like us?" Jelinek's left eye closed when he tried for a smile. "Long-term guys, gonna be in a *long* time? Why, you and me, we could spend the first ten years just gettin caught up on the old days."

"The past doesn't interest me," Parker said, and moved on.

Jelinek hopped along with him. "I bet the present interests you," he said. "I bet the future's what you talk about with Marcantoni and the schvug all the time."

Parker stopped. He looked at Jelinek. "What do you think you know?"

"I think I know you stopped," Jelinek told him. "That's one thing I think I know."

"Tell me another thing."

"They want you in Cal," Jelinek said. "Es-*cap*-ing. Killing a guard." He grinned, and the eye shut. "They hate it when you kill a guard."

"They don't mind when we kill each other," Parker told him.

"Oh, some of us, they do," Jelinek said. He was pleased with himself. "Some of us," he said, "they like to see alive, moving here and there."

Parker said, "Is there a point to this?"

"You and those boys," Jelinek said, "have travel plans." He waited for Parker to comment, but Parker merely looked at him, giving him nothing, so Jelinek shrugged and said, "You got plans, and why not? All three of you are looking at heavy time. I don't have to know what the plans are, I just have to know you got em."

"Think what you want to think."

"I do." Jelinek looked around, then pretended he was being confidential. "Me, I wanna travel, too," he said. "I been livin this life too long, I wanna settle down. You believe I got a daughter?"

"If you say so," Parker said.

"Well, I do. She's forty-one years of age, runs a nursing home in Montana. My own daughter. Would I be happy there?"

"Probably so," Parker said.

"Need help getting there, that's the thing," Jelinek explained. "Hitch a ride on a bus with somebody."

Parker waited. Jelinek squinted at him. "You boys got a bus," he said. "I don't have to know what it is, when it is, where it is, all I got to know is, you boys got a bus. And here's what I think. When you fire up that bus, I'm on it. I'm riding along with you."

Again, Jelinek waited, and again Parker simply stood and looked at him. Jelinek didn't like the lack of feedback. "Not gonna argue with me?" he demanded. "Not gonna go all innocent, you don't have any bus, you and them other two? Not gonna go all tough guy, warn me keep my mouth shut or you're gonna do all kindsa shit, and how'd I like that?"

"You've heard all that before," Parker said.

"Yes, I have," Jelinek agreed. "There isn't a goddam thing I haven't heard before, Ronnie Kasper. When that bus of yours is ready to roll, be sure to give me the word, because *some* word is going *somewhere*. Either I'm on that bus, or that bus doesn't roll."

13

We have to kill him," Marcantoni said. He was lifting the hand weights again, but bunching his arms more, because he was mad.

"Not now," Parker said. He stood by Williams' head, where Williams lay on his back on the bench, lifting and lowering the weighted bar, resting it between times on the vertical metal posts.

"The longer he's alive," Marcantoni said, "the more sure it is he'll rat us out."

"He doesn't know anything yet," Parker said. "And the guards saw him talk to me today. If he dies now, it draws attention right at us."

Williams rested the bar on the posts. "But Tom's right," he said. "He saw us together. That's what he does, he prowls around like that, looks for something he can deal in. He might not wait until he's got everything in a package."

Parker said, "What does he give them? At this point, what's he got to sell?"

"You listened to him," Marcantoni said. "That means you got something to protect."

Parker nodded. "He made the same point. But if I duck away from him, that's even worse, because then I don't know how much he's got. The reason he braced me is because he's already got his eye on us. That doesn't change. But what does he know? He knows we're long-termers and we're together, and it isn't natural for us to be together."

"Damn it," Williams said.

"So," Parker said, "he asks me questions, and I give him nothing. He'll keep watching us, try to see what we do, where we go, try to figure out what our idea is. While he's doing that, he won't talk to the guards because he doesn't have anything to give them yet."

Williams said, "You think there's any chance he really does want to come along?"

"None," Parker said.

"Jelinek doesn't want life on the run," Marcantoni said. "All he wants is to build up some merit badges, make his time on the inside easier."

Parker said, "That's right. He doesn't want to be on the outside. He's got everything he wants right in here."

"Or the place he gets sent, after his trial," Marcantoni said. "And he's angling for that place to be a nice retirement village."

"On our backs," Williams said.

"You got it."

Williams hefted the weight again, put it back. "But what we do now is nothing."

Parker said, "And watch him watching us."

"But the last thing I do before I leave this place," Marcantoni said, "I put him down."

14

When the loudspeaker said, "Kasper," next morning, the fifteenth day here, it was too early for visitors. Parker and Williams exchanged a glance, and then Parker dropped down from his bunk and walked down to the end of the line of cages, where a second guard waited. "I'm Kasper," Parker said.

No conversation. The first guard buzzed the gate open, and the second one led the way, down the clanging stairs, through the locked door into the corridor with the white line painted down the center of the floor, through the next locked door into the main building, and there the guard said, "Wait."

Parker waited. The guard turned to his left, to that first door, the one nobody ever noticed, the one that was supposed to lead to a hall down past the library and the volunteer lawyer's exit. The guard pressed a button on the wall, then spoke into a grid beside the door, and the door buzzed open. The guard gestured for Parker to go first.

This was the route. This was what he'd been wanting to see, and now that he was looking at it he realized he'd already seen it once before, from the other direction, when they'd first brought him in. At that time, he'd been concentrating too much on too many other things, hadn't paid attention to the route coming into this place because he hadn't expected he'd ever go out the same way.

But this was the way. The locked and guarded parking area was just outside this wall to the left, not only for the guards' personal cars but also for delivering fresh fish. The hall was a little narrower than the other one, with no windows, nothing on the left but a yellow-painted concrete block wall, and the same wall on the right with a gray-blue metal door in it, down toward the far end. The volunteer lawyer's door; had to be.

Parker was now completely alert, not to where he was going, but to where he was. This was the route he'd been trying to dope out, and now they were handing it to him, giving him a guided tour. He didn't know yet why, but he would remember every bit of it.

At the far end was another barred door, which another guard buzzed them through once he'd eye-balled them, and past that door was a square foyer with a jumble of exits. The metal door to the left would lead out to the parking area. Beyond the barred door to the right stretched a normal office hallway.

And straight ahead, the open doorway on the left showed the guards' locker room while the shut gray metal door on the right was marked, in black block letters, CONFERENCE.

That last was the door Parker's escorting guard knocked on. Another buzz sounded, and the guard pulled open the door with one hand while he gestured Parker inside with the other.

Inspector Turley. Same office, same man, a small bulky red-haired middleweight. He sat at the same desk and the same steno sat at the same small table in the corner.

Turley looked at Parker without expression. He said, "Come in, Kasper. Sit down."

Parker entered, the guard following, shutting the door, leaning against it. Parker sat in the same chair as before. Turley looked at him, waiting, and then said, "You do remember me, don't you?"

"Two weeks ago," Parker said. "In here."

"I told you your friend Armiston would talk if you didn't," Turley said. "Remember that?"

"Game theory," Parker said.

Turley started to smile, proud of his student, then frowned instead, realizing the student wasn't a student. He said, "Armiston's coming around, I have to tell you that."

Parker nodded.

"Nothing to say?"

"Not yet."

"All right," Turley said. "I'll tell you what the situation is, so you don't think I'm trying to play off one fella against another fella." He cocked his head, bright-eyed. "All right?"

"Fine," Parker said, because some sort of statement was required.

"So here's the situation," Turley said. "Armiston's beginning to make noises like he'd maybe come around, but so far, it's just negotiation, you know what I mean? Jerking off, in other words."

Parker didn't really care what Armiston did, because it wouldn't affect what he himself was going to do. It would be better for Armiston, maybe, to make a deal with these people, tell them whatever he knew about the guys with the plane, the customer, and then the customer's customer; though Parker doubted Armiston knew enough to be really useful.

Still, it seemed to him Armiston wasn't the sort to plot out a break for himself, particularly from a place filled with loners like this one. He was more of a team player and a follower. Also, he was probably facing nothing more than the warehouse break-in; no California, no extradition, no murder one.

In fact, now that Turley had made him think about the situation, it made sense to Parker that Armiston had already made his deal, whatever it was going to be. He'd had two weeks for it, and nothing he did or said could make things worse for Parker, so why not?

Which meant this meeting was for a different reason. Turley had something else in mind. Parker sat there and waited for it.

Turley let him wait awhile, half-smiling, and then said, "No? Still don't wanna get involved in game theory?"

"Not right now," Parker said.

Turley sat back, toying with a pencil on his desk. "You've settled in pretty good here," he said.

It's coming now, Parker thought. He said, "You don't settle in here. This is a bus depot."

"Granted," Turley said. "That's perfectly true. In fact, most people in here never really make connections with one another at all."

This is it, Parker thought. It's *Jelinek* who's started the negotiation, "beginning to make noises like he'd maybe come around," as Turley had said of Armiston. It was Jelinek who'd passed on his observations to the authorities here, so naturally they were hoping to cut out the middleman, get the story without Jelinek's help.

"But you," Turley was going on, "you surprised me, Kasper."

"Oh, yeah?"

"Yes, you did. I figured you for the silent type, not the gregarious hail-fellow sort, not the kind of fella who makes friends that easy."

Parker shrugged at that; what else?

"But here you are," Turley said, "you got a couple buddies already."

"I do?"

Turley consulted a sheet of paper on the desk in front of himself, the sheet of paper he'd been rolling that pencil on, though the consultation was clearly just a part of the play-act. Turley knew what names he was looking for. "Thomas Marcantoni," he read; or said. "Brandon Williams."

"Williams is my cellmate," Parker said. "Why be rude to a cellmate?"

"Very wise," Turley agreed. "And you play checkers with Marcantoni."

"It makes the time pass."

"And the three of you do weights together."

"Sometimes," Parker said. "You can get out of shape in here, just sit around, wait for your trial to come along. I'm still waiting on my arraignment."

With a down-turning smile, Turley said, "I think your lawyer's mostly the cause of that. I see, by the way, you weren't happy with the lawyer the court provided."

Parker said, "Mr. Sherman? He looks to me like he was overextended. I didn't want to take up a lot of his time."

Turley laughed, and it sounded real. He said, "What are you and Marcantoni and Williams up to?"

"Staying in shape," Parker said. "Passing the time."

"I hope you don't have anything else in mind," Turley said. He gave Parker his bright-bird look, then said, "Did you know this place was built seven years ago?

Would you believe that? Seven years, and already look how it's crowded."

"Too many bad people around," Parker suggested.

"That must be it," Turley agreed. "But even with this overcrowding, this situation here being less than ideal, do you know how many escapes there've been from Stoneveldt since it opened?"

"Escapes? No. Why would I want to know about escapes?"

"Zero," Turley said. He nodded to the guard. "Take Mr. Kasper back to his cell," he said.

15

We've got to do it soon," Parker said. "They'll give us a few days, just a few, but if they don't figure anything out, they'll move us, put us on three different floors."

Marcantoni looked up from the checkerboard. "I told you, Jelinek has to die."

"On our way out," Parker said. "Otherwise, he'll see us move, and start to talk."

"That, too," Marcantoni said.

16

Looks like Thursday," Parker said. "Five P.M."

Mackey nodded. "I was wondering when you'd get around to it," he said.

Thursdays, the third tier worked on its cases late in the day, starting at two-fifteen, finishing at four forty-five. At any time before four-fifteen you could decide to go down to the library, get a little work in on your case.

Jelinek didn't work on his case, not in the same way the bozos did. Thursday afternoon, just a little before four, he was almost alone in the game room, spread on his back on a couch in the corner, reading *Car & Driver*. On the wall to the left of his head was a set of shelves where the games were kept.

He looked up when he saw Parker cross the room toward him, and would have gotten to his feet except that Parker made a down-patting motion in the air; stay there, no big deal, I just want to talk with you a minute. So Jelinek put the magazine down, looked expectant, and reacted just a bit late when he saw Marcantoni moving in from the other side, not hurrying but striding, diagonally across the room toward Jelinek's feet.

"What—"

That was as far as he got before Parker's left hand closed on his windpipe and pressed him down onto the couch. Jelinek's hands snapped up to clutch at Parker's wrist, straining to lift that arm. His legs started to writhe, but then Marcantoni casually sat on his legs, reached his hand leftward past Parker, and plucked Jelinek's right hand from Parker's wrist. Pushing that hand down onto Jelinek's stomach, Marcantoni reached across himself with his free hand to pick up the magazine from Jelinek's chest and start reading it himself, one-handed. He didn't seem to notice the convulsions of Jelinek's legs beneath him or the tense quivers of Jelinek's wrist grasped in his hand.

Jelinek's eyes and mouth were all wide open. He wanted to say something that nobody wanted to hear. His left hand gave up on the wrist pressed down on his throat, and he reached up to claw at Parker's face. Parker's free right hand plucked Jelinek's hand from the air and forced it down onto the couch arm, behind Jelinek's head, just as Williams arrived. Williams hunkered down in front of the shelves, in order to study the games on offer. His left hand reached over to take Jelinek's left hand from Parker and continue to hold it tight against the arm of the couch.

Jelinek was going, his face turning red, the struggles of his limbs getting weaker. Parker watched him, waiting for the moment. They didn't want a strangulation death, with eyes bulged and tongue protruded and flesh the color of raw beef. They needed to leave something that looked more natural than that. Inmates fell asleep on these couches all the time, with so little to do. No one would try to wake him until everybody was supposed to line up for dinner.

Now. Parker lifted his hand from Jelinek's throat. Jelinek stirred, trying to breathe, to cry out, to do something to save himself. Parker clutched Jelinek's jaw in his left hand and lifted. His right hand slid under Jelinek's head, feeling the greasy hair. Both hands clamped to that head, he snapped it hard to the left. They all heard the crack.

Parker straightened, Marcantoni stood, Williams got up from the shelves of games. They all glanced around, but the few other people in the room were involved in their games or their reading.

Marcantoni sniffed. "He shit," he said.

Parker said, "Cover him with a blanket. Williams, you go first."

Williams left the game room, while Marcantoni went to the low table where a few thin gray blankets were kept folded, for when people napped in here rather than in their cells. He threw it over Jelinek, said to Parker, "See you later," and left.

"You're running it pretty close," the guard at the stairway door said, looking at his watch.

"I just thought of something might help," Parker told him.

The guard shook his head, but didn't bother to point out that nothing was going to help any of these losers in here. Turning to his radio, he clicked it on and said, "Got another librarian coming down."

"Make that the last," squawked the radio.

"Absolutely."

The guard buzzed the gate open, not bothering to look at Parker again, and Parker went down the clanging stairs for the last time. The guards below passed him on, along the standard route, and when he went into the inmates' part of the library there were only five other cons there, including Williams and Marcantoni. Williams typed something or other at one of the electric typewriters, Marcantoni was in discussion with the volunteer lawyer at the chest-high counter separating the inmates' space from the volunteer's space, and the other three cons all doggedly typed, with just a few fingers.

Parker went over to stand on line behind Marcantoni, and to hear him say to the volunteer, "I'm gonna need one of those typewriters."

"So am I," Parker said.

There were three or four different volunteer lawyers. This one was white, tall, skinny, midthirties but already balding, and wore a yellow tie that made his pale face look even paler. Now, with a look at his watch, he called over to the cons at the typewriters, "Time's up, fellas. You can come back tomorrow."

Williams said, "I just got here."

"I know you did," the volunteer assured him. "But these other three fellas."

The three fellas were used to being ordered around. Without any argument, they gathered up their materials into the folders or envelopes they used as briefcases, and one by one made ready to leave.

Meantime, Marcantoni discussed his case with the volunteer, giving him a very complex story about missing witnesses and prejudiced ex-wives. The volunteer nodded through it all, listening, taking notes, and finally the three other cons left, trailing out, all of them trying to look hopeful. The door closed behind them at last, and Marcantoni reached out across the counter to grasp the volunteer's yellow tie, yank him forward, and head-butt him so hard the volunteer slumped, eyes out of focus, and would have fallen to the floor on his side of the counter if Marcantoni hadn't kept hold of the necktie.

Williams went over to lock the corridor door as Marcantoni and Parker pulled the volunteer up far enough onto the counter to go through his pockets, pulling out wallet, thick key ring, notepad, two pens, comb, cellphone, pocket of tissues, eyeglass cleaner cloth, and a state police ID card to put on your dashboard when illegally parked.

"Jesus," the volunteer gasped, flopping draped over the counter like a fish over the gunwale, "what are you, what are you fellas, what can you, what can you possibl . . ."

They ignored him, Parker going over the counter to see what was available on the other side, while Marcantoni kept hold of the volunteer's tie and Williams took a quick scan through his wallet, then hunkered down close to the counter so he could look the volunteer in the eye and say, "Jim? You okay, Jim?"

"What?" Hearing his name both calmed the volunteer and focused him, so that he quit flopping around and blinked at Williams. "What did you say?"

Williams tapped the open wallet, showing it to the volunteer. "Says here you're gonna be an organ donor, Jim," he said. "That's a wonderful thing, I want you to know that."

"Yes," the volunteer said, still trying to catch up.

"I mean it, Jim," Williams told him, while Parker went through the rear half of the library. "Being an organ donor's just about the most generous thing a person can do."

"It's the least," the volunteer said. He was still groggy, but focusing more on Williams now.

"No, it's the most, man," Williams insisted. "That you want to be an organ donor." He leaned closer, almost nose to nose with the volunteer. Low-voiced, confidential, he said, "But not today, Jim."

The volunteer flinched, and Marcantoni had to yank him down again by the necktie. Wide-eyed, the volunteer stared at Williams. "I don't want to die!"

"Of course you don't, Jim." Williams went on in that low, soft, confidential manner, saying, "These two guys I'm with, I've got to tell you, they're the meanest people I ever met in my life. I come along because they asked me to, and whatever they ask me to do I'm gonna do, you know what I mean? Jim? Do you know what I mean?"

"Yes," said the volunteer.

"Now, listen, Jim," Williams said. "I made these boys promise me one thing before we started. I made them promise me no killing, unless it's absolutely necessary. I mean, none of us have guns, and *you* don't have a gun, and any guard that comes in here, *they* don't carry guns, not in the part where the cons are."

"That's right," the volunteer said.

"So there won't be any killing," Williams assured him, "there won't even be any danger for anybody, if we all just stay calm and do it by the book. And Jim, what I mean here is *their* book. They're gonna ask you to do a couple things pretty soon, nothing bad, nothing hard to do. Jim, I want you to promise me, you're not gonna make me look bad. Just do what these fellas say, and you'll be outa this mess in no time."

The volunteer nodded. "I know what you're saying," he said. He sounded better now.

Parker walked back toward the counter. "There's a chair back here."

"I think Jim would like to sit awhile," Williams said.

"Time," Marcantoni said.

"Oh, you're right," Williams said. "Jim, I'm not gonna steal your watch, but I would like to look at it. Could you twist your arm around here? Thanks. It's twelve minutes to five. You gonna be okay if Tom lets go of your tie?"

"Yes," said the volunteer, so Marcantoni released the tie and the volunteer slid backward off the counter until his feet were on the floor, then stood there reeling a bit, holding to the counter edge with both hands.

Williams, sounding concerned, said, "Your vision a little blurry, Jim?"

"Yes."

"What you've got there," Williams told him, "you've got a slight concussion. Nothing serious. But when this is done, just a few minutes from now, you'll take my advice, you go straight to your family doctor. Not the ones in the dispensary here, they're not that good, if you want the truth. You go to your family doctor, right?"

"Yes," the volunteer said.

Marcantoni said, "Have somebody drive you. Don't drive yourself."

Williams said, "Good thinking."

While Parker looked around the back library area

for anything useful, he listened to Williams and Marcantoni herd the volunteer. They knew how to go about it, hard and soft, a menace but not quite a mortal threat. He'd needed to find a crew in this place, and he'd found one.

Williams said, "Jim, whyn't you sit down in your chair."

The volunteer made it across the clear space from the counter to his small desk and chair, tucked away in a corner out of sight of anybody in the inmates' area. He dropped there, both forearms on the desk, mouth slightly open.

Marcantoni was fooling with the volunteer's cellphone. Now he said, "How do I get this thing to work?"

"It doesn't work in here," the volunteer told him. "You have to take it outside."

"Well, that's where I'm going," Marcantoni said, but when he and Williams hoisted themselves over the counter he left the cellphone behind with the rest of the volunteer's stuff.

Parker told them, "There's cartons back here. Some kind of legal boxes."

"Good," Marcantoni said, looking at them. Stacked in a corner were four empty white cardboard cartons with separate cardboard tops, like the boxes used to carry evidence into court. They'd most likely been used here to bring books in.

Williams said, "What have we got for persuasion?"

"This desk lamp," Marcantoni said, and picked up from in front of the volunteer a heavy metal lamp with a pen trough in its broad base and a long green glass globe around the bulb. Marcantoni yanked the end of the cord from the outlet, then took the base of the lamp in one hand and its neck in the other and jerked them back and forth against each other until something snapped. Then he started to separate them and said, "Damn the cord. Jim, you got scissors?"

"In the top drawer," the volunteer said. He looked mournfully at his lamp.

Opening the drawer, taking out the scissors, Williams told the volunteer, "They still make those lamps, the state'll buy you another one." Turning, he snipped the cord, so Marcantoni could drop the glass globe in the wastebasket and heft the base. With a conspiratorial grin at the volunteer, Williams put the scissors back in the drawer and shut it.

Meantime, Parker had found the supplies closet; a metal stand-alone armoire with two doors on the front. Inside were mostly forms, papers, various kinds of tape. But on one shelf was a green metal file box, sixteen inches long, meant for 3x5 cards. It was full of the cards, half in use for various records, the rest still in their clear packaging. The file box was unwieldy, but heavy; Parker ran duct tape over the front of it, to keep it closed, so he could carry it by the front handle.

Williams said, "Is it time?"

"Might as well," Marcantoni said.

Williams sat on the corner of the volunteer's desk. "Jim," he said, "this is where you've got to do it right, or you're in big trouble."

The volunteer looked at him, tense, waiting.

"You're gonna call out to the guards at the end of the corridor," Williams told him. "The way you do every day, phone to them to unlock your door here so you can go home. But today you're gonna tell them you've got two heavy cartons of law books to be carried out of here, and you'd appreciate it if a couple guards could come down and give you a hand. You've done that kind of thing before, the guards carrying the heavy stuff for the civilians like you, am I right?"

"Sometimes," the volunteer said.

"And today is one of those times. Do you want me to repeat the story," Williams asked him, "or do you have it?"

"Oh, I have it," the volunteer said. He sounded very depressed. He said, "Please don't kill them, they're just working guys."

"Come on, Jim," Williams said, "nobody's gonna kill nobody, I already told you that. Because we're all gonna do our part. So if we all do our part, why should there be any extra mess?"

"More trouble for you," the volunteer suggested.

"Exactly! Do it now, Jim, while the story's fresh in your mind. Pick up the phone."

The volunteer picked up the phone. Williams gently

touched a finger to the back of the hand holding the phone, and the volunteer flinched. His voice softer than ever, Williams said, "But just remember, Jim. If you do anything at all except what I told you, anything at all, then I'm sorry. You're an organ donor."

Jim did very well.

17

The guards were one white and one black, which was useful but not necessary. Their replacements wouldn't be standing around for inspection.

Williams crouched under the little desk, where he could come out fast into the volunteer's back if it looked as though he were coming unstuck. Parker and Marcantoni waited around on the far side of the supplies closet, its one door opened out in front of them, the stacked cartons just a few feet away across the room.

"It's the top two there," the volunteer said, pointing at the boxes, hanging back to hold the door ajar the way Williams had whispered just before the guards got here. He sounded nervous and shaky, but not too much so.

"No problem," the white guard said, and they moved forward, the white first, reaching for the top box, jerking upward with it in surprise when it didn't carry the expected weight, saying, "This is—" He would have said "light," but Parker and Marcantoni came boiling out from behind them, Parker swinging the file box at the white head, Marcantoni aiming at the black.

The guards were big guys, and strong. Both went down to their knees when they were hit, but neither of them was out. Standing in the middle of the room, with more space to swing and aim, Parker and Marcantoni slammed those two heads again, and the guards dropped.

Parker spun away as the volunteer recoiled, letting the hall door go, Williams coming fast out from under the desk to jam a book into the opening to keep the door from closing itself completely, which would automatically lock them in again. Pointing at the volunteer, voice low and fast, Parker said, "Give me your clothes."

The volunteer stared at Parker in owlish surprise. "But you're a lot bigger than I am."

"Tom's bigger," Parker told him, "so it's me." He was already peeling off his jeans. "Come on, Jim."

Marcantoni and Williams ripped off their own jeans and stripped the guards, then put on their uniforms. Keeping his own T-shirt, Parker forced himself into the volunteer's slacks, shirt, yellow tie and sports jacket. He looked like something from a silent comedy when he was done, but nobody would have a lot of time to study him.

The volunteer stood there in his undershirt and shorts and socks and shoes, holding Parker's jeans in both hands as though not sure what they were. The others were ready. Parker moved to his right, away from the others, and whispered, "Jim."

Jim turned his head, and Marcantoni cracked the lamp base across the back of his head. Parker broke his fall, to keep him from making a racket, while the other two each picked up one of the empty boxes, carrying it high as though it were full and heavy, obscuring whatever was ill-fitting about their uniforms or wrong about their faces. Parker followed, trusting the two large men in front of him to keep him from too close inspection.

The empty hall. At the far end, as they approached, the door was buzzed open. Straight ahead was the conference room, where Inspector Turley sometimes lurked. To the right was the civilian office space. To the left was the parking lot.

A volunteer lawyer and, later, two guards had walked in. Now the same seemed to come back out, doing what was expected of them, turning left after the first door. The two guards on duty, hardly noticing them at all, buzzed them through and they went out that final door to the parking lot.

The door slid shut behind them. "Walk toward the gate," Parker said.

The big square blacktop area, surrounded by its high walls on three sides, was half full, haphazardly parked with Corrections buses and private cars. The gate, on the fourth side, a tall electronically run chain-link rectangle with razor wire along the top, was to their right. They walked toward it.

Marcantoni said, "They should be here." He sounded very tense, holding the box too tight, so that it might crumble in his hands.

"They'll wait to see us," Parker said.

They kept walking, not in a hurry. Parker was aware of guard towers up and behind them, of eyes casually on them but on them. They kept walking, diagonally toward the gate, the two guards carrying the big white boxes high like offerings, followed by the ill-dressed attorney. Beyond the gate were farmland and woods. No traffic.

A blue-black van appeared in the road beyond the chain-link gate. It angled to the gate and jolted to a stop and honked, as the driver leaned out to shout into a speaker mounted on a metal pole out there. "I'm late, goddamit!" Parker heard Mackey yell, and saw that the van had STATE CORRECTIONS ID on its side door.

Slow, ponderous, the gate began to slide open. Somebody behind them at the building began to yell. With the widening of the gate barely broad enough, the van nosed itself through, scraping against the fixed post on its left side.

More shouting. The van was half in and half out, the gate jerking to a stop as the side door of the van slid open.

"Now!" Parker yelled, and the three ran for the van, hurling away the boxes, a flurry of firecrackers going off behind them, Mackey already backing out as they dove headfirst through the side opening onto the metal floor.

Struggling upward as the van jounced and its side door slammed shut, Parker stared out the meshed rear window as Mackey backed them in a tight U-turn, then jammed them forward. The gate back there was closing again, just as slow, just as certain, but too late. It stopped. Before it could open once more, to permit pursuit, Mackey had taken a forested curve on two wheels and Stoneveldt was out of sight.

TWO

1

When Williams got his rump under him and hands braced on the floor, the van was leaping down a road and sharply around a left turn. There were six of them in here, he the only black; not good. The three who'd come with the van wore dark shirts and jackets and military-style billed caps, to give them the look of Corrections personnel. One of them drove, a second beside him, and the third sat in back with the escapees; he was the one who'd opened and shut the side door.

There were no seats back here, only thin gray carpet over the metal floor. Williams and Kasper and Marcantoni and the fourth man sat cross-legged on the floor, holding on to whatever they could find, and the driver worked to put a lot of distance between them and Stoneveldt.

After a minute, Williams noticed that the new guy back here was frowning at him, as though not sure what to do about him. Thinking, let's work this out right away, Williams gave Kasper a flat look and waited. Kasper looked back at him, then told the new one, "We're all traveling together."

The new one switched his gaze to Kasper, thought a second, then nodded. "Fine with me," he said. "You're Parker."

"And this is Williams."

"I'm Jack Angioni." He nodded, accepting them both, then pointed his jaw at the passenger up front. "And that's Phil Kolaski."

"Hold tight," the driver said, and took them on a screaming right turn onto a twisty narrow black-top road.

Bracing himself against the driver's seatback, Angioni said, "Most of the roads around here you can see from the prison. See for miles, with all these open plains. We had to do a tricky route, to keep in the cover of the trees."

"It's all flat and open around here," the driver called from up front. "It's disgusting, Parker, I don't know why you ever came out here."

Kolaski, the heel of one hand pressed to the dash-board, half-turned to say, "We got one more turn for Mackey to try to kill us, and then we ditch this thing."

"Good," Marcantoni said. "My bones don't like this seat."

Kasper—or Parker, maybe—said, "Mackey, what about clothes?"

"In the next cars," the driver—Mackey—told him. "Hold on, here's the turn Phil likes."

There was a tractor trailer coming the other way, that a lot of people would have waited for; in fact, the driver of the rig kept coming as though he thought Mackey would wait. But Mackey spun the wheel, accelerated hard, and shot leftward past the nose of the truck into another narrow road through forest. The driver of the truck bawled his airhorn at them, but the noise quickly fell away, and Kolaski half-turned again to say, "That was a little quicker than in the practice."

Mackey said, "I didn't have that semi there in the practice."

Angioni said, "Ed, no stunts on the dirt road, okay? Dust, remember? You can see it rise up in the air, miles away."

"No dust," Mackey promised, and tapped the brake a few times, slowing them before they made a gentle right turn onto rutted one-lane dirt.

They moved more slowly now, but the jouncing was worse. They did half a mile like that, surrounded by slender-trunked trees, and then on their left was a body of water instead, gleaming in late-afternoon sun, a few feet below the road. Williams looked past Mackey and out the windshield and saw it was a good-size lake, with some sort of structure far ahead, where the shore curved.

Parker said, "What is this?"

"Swimming up there in the summer," Angioni told him. "Nothing, this time of year."

Mackey braked to a stop. "Right here," he said.

They all climbed out of the van, stretching, everybody stiff. Williams saw that the road, which had been ten feet or so from the lake before this, had now curved closer, so the water was just there, below the side of the road.

Mackey and Kolaski peeled off their hats and jackets, tossing them through open windows into the van. Then Mackey said, "Drop it any time. We'll be back." And he and Kolaski walked away down the dirt road toward the swimming place.

Angioni had also stripped off his hat and jacket. "The water's deep here," he said. "A lot better than trying to clean this thing."

Williams and Marcantoni stripped off the upper parts of the uniforms, while Parker did the same with the lawyer's jacket and tie and shirt, all the clothing tossed into the van. Then Angioni backed the van in a half-circle, drove it forward to the lakeside edge of the road, put it in Neutral, and climbed down.

The four of them got behind the van and pushed, and lazily it rolled off the road, its rear end abruptly jumping upward, then sliding at an angle down and away. The van went into the water deliberately, almost reluctantly, air bubbling up from the open windows; then all at once it dropped below the level they could see, and there was only the water, still and black. Not even bubbles any more.

Williams stepped back, behind the others watching the van sink, wondering if he was supposed to be next now. But they turned without menace, Parker looking away in the direction the other two had gone, while Marcantoni grinned and made a remark into the air about the parking of the van. So maybe it was going to be all right.

Brandon Williams had grown used to this level of tension, never knowing exactly how to react to the people around him, who and what to watch for, where it was safe to put a foot. Part of it was skin color, but the rest was the life he'd lived, usually on the bent. He'd had square jobs, but they'd never lasted. He'd always known the jobs were beneath him, that he was the smartest man on the job site or the factory floor, but that it didn't matter how smart he was, or how much he knew, or the different things he'd read. The knowledge would make him arrogant and angry, and sooner or later there'd be a fight, or he'd be fired.

The people he mostly got along with were, like him, on the wrong side of the law. It wasn't that they were smart, most of them, but that they kept to themselves. He got along with people who kept to themselves; that way, he could keep to himself, too.

And to his own kind. The jobs he pulled, suburban banks, places like that, didn't need a big gang; two or three men, usually. There'd been times when one of the crew was white, but not often.

Twice in his life he'd taken falls, but both were minor, and he'd wound up spending a total of fifty-seven months inside. But this time was different.

He'd known he was making a mistake when he'd agreed to team up with Eldon. The more you stayed away from junkies, the better off you'd be. But Maryenne had pleaded, had sworn Eldon was better now, just needed the kind of self-confidence he'd get if Williams agreed to work with him, and Williams had never been able to refuse his youngest sister, so when he went into that bank, Eldon was next to him. The third man, Haye, was in the car outside.

Maryenne herself wasn't a junkie, at least Williams hoped she wasn't, but she sure hung out with the wrong people, and Eldon was still one of them. The kind of self-confidence he brought into the bank was not the kind he'd get from working with Williams but the kind he'd get from the stuff in his veins. There was no reason to start shooting, and just bad luck the off-duty cop was in there looking for a car loan.

The result was, a guard and Eldon both dead and Williams and Haye both facing murder one. Escape was the only Plan B, and this guy Parker the only one in Stoneveldt with the determination and the friends on the outside to make it happen.

Williams had been happy to stick with Parker in Stoneveldt, though he would have been more comfortable if his partner had been of color. But nobody of color in that place looked to be making a key to get out of there, and Parker did. So when Parker asked him to come along, he rode with the idea, though at first with every caution. Does this guy really want a partner, or does he want somebody to throw off the sled when the chase starts?

Throughout their time together inside, Williams had watched the man he'd known then as Kasper, waiting for him to give himself away, and it never happened. It looked as though Parker was just a guy determined to get out of that place, who'd known he couldn't do it on his own but needed a couple more guys in it with him, and who'd decided Williams should be part of the crew. No more, no less.

Well, that was then, this was now. They were out, though still not many miles from Stoneveldt. But guards and gates and prison walls didn't hold them apart any more. Williams watched Parker, thinking, I done my part, I been straight with you. I know you got me out of there, but I got you out of there, too, so what does that mean? Is this crew still together?

He was dependent on Parker, whichever way he went. It wasn't possible to ask anything, so all he could do was stand there and watch and wait, and know that, sooner or later, they would both be going to ground, but in very different places.

While they all stood there, looking at the water where the van had been, nobody with anything else to say right now, here came two cars, both anonymous, a green Ford Taurus and a black Honda Accord. Mackey was first, at the wheel of the Taurus. Both cars stopped, and Angioni said, "You two ride with Ed, he knows where we're going. See you there."

Parker slid into the front passenger seat, Williams into the back. On the seat was a little bundle of clothing. As Mackey drove them forward, Williams slipped out of his shoes and the prison guard's pants, and put on instead gray chinos and a green patterned shirt. In front, Parker made a similar changeover.

As they headed on down the dirt road, back the way they'd come in, the Honda following, Williams moved forward to put his forearms on the seatback behind the other two, and watch the road. No one said anything until after they'd reached the blacktop and turned right, and then Parker said, "Did Tom tell you about this new job?"

Mackey grinned. "My guess was," he said, "you weren't gonna like it, not at first. You and Brenda and me, we want to be in some other part of the world."

"That's what makes sense," Parker agreed.

Williams supposed that was what made sense for him, too, the way things were. He was a local boy, who had made a little too good. As soon as possible, he should ease out to some other part of the country. It's a big country, and a black boy can make himself hard to see.

Mackey was saying, "It isn't a bad job. We should be

able to work it without problems, and at least we'll get off this tabletop with a little cash profit."

Williams said, "This is a cash job? It's tough to find real cash, I mean, enough to make it worthwhile."

"No, it's jewelry," Mackey told him. "But they've got a buyer, in New Orleans, he'll drive up as soon as we do the job, we'll have cash a day later."

Parker said, "From a jewelry store?"

"It's not a jewelry store," Mackey said, "it's a wholesaler. He's the one sells to the jewelry stores, all around this flat part of the world here."

They were coming into the city now, with more traffic, with stop signs and traffic lights. Parker said, "This is going to be right in the middle of town."

"You know it," Mackey said.

"Will we go past it now?"

"No, it's more downtown. Where we're headed now used to be a beer distributor. Just a few blocks up here."

This neighborhood was old commercial, little office buildings and manufacturing places and delivery outfits, mostly brick, all seedy. Evening was coming on, traffic moderate, mostly small trucks and vans. The Honda kept a steady distance behind them.

After another block, Parker said, "The reason they put us in front, it's in case we change our mind."

Mackey laughed. "What would they do, do you think," he asked, "if I suddenly hit a turn, took off?"

"We're not going to," Parker said.

Mackey was making Williams nervous. People who

didn't take serious things seriously always made him nervous. Junkies were like that. Mackey wasn't a junkie, but he had the style. Williams, forearms on the seatback, looked at Mackey in the interior mirror. "I don't think this is the time to do jokes," he said.

Mackey grinned in the mirror. "You tell me when," he said.

2

Tom Marcantoni was pleased with the place Jack and Phil had found. In a low-rent neighborhood of factories and warehouses, no private homes, this two-story brick building was one huge open space inside, concrete-floored, big enough for three delivery trucks and who knew how many cases and barrels of beer. The company had been absorbed by a bigger distributor, making this building redundant, and no one had another use for it yet. Electric and water were still on, Jack and Phil had put cots in the offices upstairs, and so long as they were reasonably cautious they shouldn't attract attention.

Phil steered the Honda into the building, behind the Taurus, and both cars stopped. Jack jumped out to close the big overhead door, all the others climbed out and stretched, and Marcantoni got out at a more leisurely pace, grinning.

He couldn't help it. It was all back on track. To

think, just a few days ago, he'd thought he was screwed forever, put away like a goldfish in a bowl.

From the minute he'd gone inside, he'd been hoping and looking and waiting for a way to break that bowl, but Parker had been right: You couldn't do it alone. So now he had these new partners, solid guys he could count on, and he still had the old score, waiting for him, downtown.

It had taken a while to be sure Williams and Kasper—or Parker now, or whoever he was—would stand up. Williams had been easier for Angioni and Kolaski to check up on, being a local boy, and the word had come back that he was sound; for a nigger, very good. For anybody, in fact, very good; cool in the action and never too greedy.

As for Parker, it had been easier for Kolaski to get a handle on his pal, Ed Mackey. Mackey had a good reputation back east, a lot like Williams, but Parker was a more shadowy figure, showing up here and there, solid but dangerous. The word was, after a while, that you could count on him but you had to be wary of him, too. If he got the idea you planned to cross him, he didn't take prisoners.

Well, that was all right. Marcantoni was also not too greedy, and smart enough not to make trouble inside his own crew. There was plenty in this job for everybody. He wouldn't cross Parker, and Parker wouldn't cross him, so neither of them had anything to worry about.

And finally, the best recommendation for Parker

was that Mackey would go out of his way for him, be the outside man when it came time to break out of Stoneveldt. Marcantoni would do that for Angioni and Kolaski, and they would for him—they'd just done it—so that was all the guarantee you needed.

There was still a little of the old furniture in the building, including a long table and some folding chairs next to one of the long brick walls. Apparently, this was where the drivers would fill out their forms, get their requisitions and their routes. Now, the six of them crossed to this table, Jack Angioni leading the way for the new guys and Marcantoni just naturally taking his place at the head.

When everybody was seated, he grinned around at them all and said, "I waited six years for this job, and it was beginning to look as though I was gonna have to wait sixty, but here we are. Ed, did these two fill you in?"

"Halfway," Ed Mackey said.

"Okay, then, I'll do it from the top." Talking mostly to Parker and Williams, he said, "Six seven years ago, I was on parole, I had to have a day job, I worked construction here in town. Downtown there's this big old armory building, brick, from Civil War days. The army still used it for like National Guard and shit until the sixties. Then it just sat there. Every once in a while, the city would borrow it and use the parade field in there—indoor, hardwood floor, you know what I mean—for a charity ball, something like that."

Ed Mackey said, "There's old armories like that all over the country."

Marcantoni nodded. "And we got this one. And finally the government decided to turn a dollar on the thing, and they sold it to some local developers. It's a big building, it's a city block square. They put some high-ticket apartments on the upper floors, with views out over the city and the plains and all, but it was tough to know what to do with the main floor, where the parade field was. The outside walls were four feet thick, with little narrow deep windows, ready to repel an attack like if the Indians had tanks. You couldn't put street-level shops in there, nobody wanted an apartment down in there, and even for a bank it was too grim."

Williams said, "I was in there sometimes when I was a kid. They used it for track and field. I remember, it was like a fort."

"It *is* a fort," Marcantoni told him. "That's the point. One of the developers was a guy named Henry Freedman, got his money from his father's wholesale jewelry business, which was on two floors of an office building downtown, upper floors for the security but a pain in the ass for the salesmen and the deliveries. So they worked it out, they'd lease part of the main floor of the armory to Freedman's father, he'd move his wholesale business in there; on the street, but even more secure than the office building. The rest of the space they leased to some dance studio."

Parker said, "You worked on the refit."

"That's just right," Marcantoni said. "And I found the secret entrance."

That got the blank looks he'd anticipated. He said, "I looked it up afterward, that's what they used to do. Like they're getting ready for a siege, they put in a little back entrance nobody knows about."

Flat, Williams said, "A secret entrance."

"No, it's true," Marcantoni told him. "I had free time on the job there, I liked to poke around, see what was what, and there was this locked metal door in the basement, no knob, just a keyhole. I wondered, what's back there? Maybe government gold, everybody forgot about it. So I managed a look at the blueprints in the site office, and there was no door there. It wasn't on the plans."

Williams said, "Did you get it open?"

"Sure. I took a bar down, and popped two bricks next to the door so I could pull it open, and I put my flashlight in there, and it was a tunnel, brick all around, like five feet wide, maybe six feet high, going straight out."

Williams said, "To where?"

"A pile of trash, blocking it," Marcantoni told him. "Part of the thing fell in some time, who knows when. So I put the door back, put the bricks back, and later I figured out where it had to go, if it was a straight line, and it had to go to the library across Indiana Avenue.

That was the first public library here, federal money, built around the same time as the armory."

Parker said, "You looked over there."

"I had to break into the library," Marcantoni said. "But libraries are not tough to break into. I went in three nights, and I finally found it, with storage shelves built up in front of it. They didn't know anything about it either. I got through that door, and went along the tunnel as far as where it was broken in, and I don't think there can be more than five or ten feet where it's blocked. You know, they pulled up the trolley tracks along there maybe fifty years ago, it could be they screwed up the tunnel then, never knew they did it."

Parker said, "Your idea is, we go in there, clear it, have all night in the wholesaler's."

Marcantoni grinned, he was so pleased with the whole thing. He said, "I told myself, wait at least five years, so nobody's thinking about the crews did the makeover."

Williams said, "How do you know, when you're pulling that rubble out of the way, there won't be some more come down? I don't like the idea of tunnels that already fell in once."

"It's only that one short part," Marcantoni assured him. "My idea is, we'll take two or three of those long tables from the reading room in the library, they're not far away. We clear stuff, shove the tables ahead of us, we go on all fours under them, just that one part of the route. Anything else falls down, they're sturdy tables, they'll keep it clear."

Williams said, "Guns. Alarms."

"I can tell you about that," Phil Kolaski said. "I was looking into it before Tom tripped. Because the building's so solid, the only way into the jewelry place—"

"The only way they *think*," Marcantoni corrected.

"Sure," Kolaski agreed. "But that is what they think. The front door on the street, that's all they worry about. There's three separate entrances, for the jewelry operation, the dance studio, the apartments upstairs. They're right next to each other, and there's a doorman around the clock for the apartments. The dance studio just has a couple regular locks, you could go in that way except for the doorman. The jewelry operation has an alarmed front door *plus* a barred gate *plus* an articulated steel door comes down over the whole thing."

Williams said, "No motion sensors inside."

"They really don't expect anybody inside," Kolaski said. "Except through that front door. It *looks* solid."

There was a little pause and then Williams said, "What are the hours, in this library?"

Marcantoni answered that one: "Sunday they close at five P.M."

Angioni said, "And Sunday, the jeweler isn't open at all."

Williams said, "You want to do it this Sunday, or a week and a half from now?"

"This Sunday," Marcantoni said. "Who wants to hang around?"

"Nobody," Parker said.

3

When he heard the first news on his police scanner, Goody popped a call to Maryenne, cellphone to cellphone. "You home?"

"No, I'm at the family center."

All the mamas read to their babies at the family center. "Read to him tomorrow," Goody said. "I'll meet you your place. I got news for you."

"What news?"

"Tell ya when I see ya, lovey," Goody said, and broke the connection, because this wasn't the kind of news you'd talk about, chat away, back and forth, on a *cellphone*, where any fool in the world can be listening in.

Goody shut off the scanner, started the Mercury, and drove away from the post where he'd been sitting the last hour and a half, one of the few cars moving in this miserable slum neighborhood. Three blocks later he made a left onto a one-way street and stopped next to the Land Rover parked at the left curb, where Buck sat in the backseat with his two bodyguards up front. The bodyguards eyeballed him, but they knew Goody, and looked down the street again instead.

Goody lowered his window and Buck did the same thing on the other side, saying, "You leavin early? Somethin wrong back there?"

"No, I got a family emergency," Goody told him. He picked up the shopping bag from between his feet, with the merchandise and the money in it, and passed it over to Buck. "I'll be back tomorrow, same as ever."

"I didn't hear nothin on the scanners," Buck said. He frowned like he was trying to work out what he should be suspicious about.

"No, I got it on my cell," Goody told him, and raised the phone from the seat to show it. "Family business," he said. "See you tomorrow."

Buck wouldn't recognize that name, Brandon Williams, one of the three hardcases that had just bust out of Stoneveldt outside town, leaving behind them one dead inmate and a lot of aching heads. Buck wouldn't know it, what had all those police dispatchers talking so fast, ordering this car that way, that car this way, but Goody would. And where else would old Brandon go now, when he had to lay as low as a footprint, except to his sister Maryenne? And where else would Goody go, to see the boy?

Maryenne lived in a third floor back with her grandmother and her sister and her sister's boyfriend and her baby Vernon and her sister's two babies. Maryenne didn't have a boyfriend right now that Goody knew of, so he thought he might move in for a while, see how that would play, make life easy while he waited for old Brandon.

When he got there and knocked on the door—the street door downstairs wasn't locked because the push-buttons in the apartments hadn't worked for thirty years—it was opened by a short heavy girl with a baby on her hip. "I'm Goody," he told her. "Maryenne's expecting me."

She gave him the look she probably gave every man since she got the baby—I know your type, keep your distance—and said, "If she's expecting you, come on in."

He went on in, and the living room was full of them, young mamas and their babies. It looked as though Maryenne had brought her whole reading group from the family center, and maybe that was supposed to be a hint to Goody that she wasn't of a mood for romance, but that was okay. He could be the friend of the family, work just as well, be there in moments of need, like when old Brandon showed his face.

It wasn't only that Maryenne had her whole reading group here, they'd all brought their books, too, and there they were, all over the room, on the couch and the chairs and the floor, babies in their laps, books in their hands, reading out loud. They were all quiet about it, but there sure were a lot of them, and it reminded him of the sound of the pigeons on the roof, in a big cage room that had been on top of one of the buildings where he'd lived when he was a kid, ten or eleven years ago. The guy that owned the pigeons was a bus driver, and he didn't mind if Goody or some of the other kids came up there with him sometimes, hang out with the pigeons. He and his wife didn't have any kids of their own, Goody remembered.

Huh; maybe that was why he had the pigeons.

Maryenne was in a chair by the switched-off TV set, Vernon in her lap. Vernon was about a year old now, and Goody couldn't for the life of him see what the point was in mamas reading to babies that little that they didn't know anything yet, but it was supposed to do some kind of good or another and everybody believed in it, so maybe so. Vernon was going to need all the help he could get anyway; his papa was Eldon, who'd got himself killed in that bank he was in with old Brandon. The one thing Goody definitely didn't ever want Maryenne to know was that he'd been Eldon's dealer, including on that final day.

"Say there," Goody said, and walked around a lot of mamas and babies to grin at Maryenne up close. She was a nice girl, a lot younger than old Brandon, he being their mama's first and Maryenne being her last.

She was nice, and she was young, but she also had that same look on her face as the one that had opened the door to him. "You got some kind of news, Goody?" she asked him.

The news was going to be known by everybody in

this room, and in this city, soon enough, but Goody wanted it to start off a special secret just between the two of them; the beginning of that closeness he'd need until old Brandon showed up. So he said, "Come on in the kitchen, Maryenne, let me tell you just you."

"There's nothing you can't tell me here," she said. She still held the book up—thin, bright colors, called *The Very Red Butterfly*—like she wanted Goody done and gone so she could get back to reading, like she was in a hurry to know how the story would come out.

He put a solemn face on and said, "I think you'd want me to tell this to just you, Maryenne."

So then she treated him a little more seriously, becoming worried, saying, "Is it something bad?"

"You tell me. Come on, girl."

Fretful, she got to her feet, dropping the book on her chair, moving Vernon over onto her hip. He would have preferred to talk with her without Vernon, but he realized it would be pushing his luck to try for that, so he just led the way through the cooing mamas out the door, down the hall, and on down to the kitchen doorway, where he stopped, because the grandmother was in there, seated at the kitchen table, reading an astrology magazine.

Goody turned back. "We'll talk here," he said, keeping his voice low, and moving so he'd be out of the grandmother's sight, away from the doorway.

Maryenne was burning with curiosity and worry: "What is it, Goody? Come *on*."

"Brandon," he said. "Him and two other guys, they just bust outa the jail."

She stared at him. She didn't seem to know how to react, except to stare at his face, as though to memorize it. Even Vernon stopped his usual gnawing on his fist to look at Goody, his expression thoughtful and a little skeptical.

"Maryenne? You hear what I said?"

"It was that man," she said. She sounded awed.

He frowned at her. "What man?"

"Chili Greebs brought him around," she said. Chili Greebs owned a bar not far from here, was in and out of different kinds of businesses. She said, "A white man. Chili said he was all right, and I was supposed to pass on a message to Brandon when I visited, that there was a white man in there with him named Kasper that he could trust."

"Huh," Goody said.

"But I thought it was just to help each other in there," she said. "I didn't know they meant *this*."

Goody said, "You know what it means, don't you?"

"They're gonna kill him." she whispered.

"Waddaya mean, kill him?" Goody demanded. "That's not what's gonna happen."

"They're gonna hunt him down," she whispered, "and they're gonna kill him." Her eyes were filling.

"No, but that's why I come here," Goody told her. "Cause we can help. You and me, with you and me on the case, they're never gonna find him."

Finally he had her attention. Frowning, she said, "What do you mean, you and me?"

"Where's he gonna come?" Goody asked her. "He's gonna need help now, lie low, get out of this state, probly get outa the whole country, get to Mexico, South America, somewhere. He can't do that on his own, and who's he gonna turn to? His favorite sister, that's who. There's no place else he's gonna turn."

She thought about it. "He'll call," she decided. "He won't come here, because they'd catch him, but he'll call."

"And that's when," Goody said, "you send him to me."

"To you? Why to you?"

"Don't you think the cops're gonna be keepin an eye on you? Don't you think they know who you are, where you are? But you're right, Brandon's gonna call, and when he does, you send him to me, cause the cops don't know about *me*, and we can work it out together."

She was frowning again. She said, "Why you wanna do that?"

"Cause I always liked old Brandon," he told her. "And I always liked you. And I was playing with my police scanners, and I heard the first report, so I know I'm ahead of the news here, and you and me can plot and plan before anybody else even *knows* anything."

She nodded, thinking about it. Then she said, "It's for sure, now. He broke out."

"It'll be on the news," he told her, "the first anybody

else knows about it. It'll be on the news. What time is it? Half an hour, it'll be on the news."

"Poor Brandon," she said.

"He'll call you, you know he will."

Slowly she nodded. "Yes, he will."

"And you send him to me. Maryenne? You send him to me."

"All right," she said.

"Good."

"Thank you, Goody," she said.

"Oh, I knew I had to do it," he assured her. "Soon as I heard that police report, I knew I had to be on hand, I had to help old Brandon somehow."

Yes, and by then, for certain sure, there would be a very nice reward out on good old Brandon's head.

4

The class was called Low Impact Rhythm and was theoretically a preliminary for classes in ballroom dancing, but was actually merely an exercise class with slower music. In addition to Brenda, there were eleven other students here this evening, nine women and two men, and of them all, if she did say so herself, she was the youngest, the fittest, and the cutest. She didn't *need* to take some flab off her ass, like that one over there, or learn not to move like an elephant on downers, like that one over there. Watching herself in the side-wall mirror, echoing herself echoing the instructor, a whippet-thin black man in black leotards, she knew she was already at what this class was supposed to move you toward.

The mirror was twenty feet long and eight feet high in this long room, with barres on the end walls, a piano (ignored) at one side, and soundproofing in the ceiling to keep the reverb down. Brenda was interested in the mirror not only for what she saw in it, her own cute ass, firm body, rhythmic movements, but also for what she couldn't see beyond it.

This hardwood floor she and the group were step-step-stepping on was part of the parade field from the building's military days. The field, she knew, continued on under the mirrored wall. Over there, imaginable in her mind's eye, was the jewelry wholesaler, like something out of the Arabian Nights. Another reason to smile at the mirror.

When she traveled with Ed Mackey, Brenda called herself Brenda Fawcett. Since she seemed to travel with Ed all the time, she might as well *be* Brenda Fawcett, so a while ago, for a birthday present, Ed had given her various kinds of ID—driver's licenses from different states, credit cards she shouldn't try to use— all in that name. What made it a real present was, all the IDs made her a year younger.

She'd called herself Brenda Fawcett here at the Johnson-Ross Studio of the Dance out of habit. She wouldn't be flashing ID here because she was paying for her lessons—this was the third—in cash, explaining to the receptionist at the initial interview, showing a smile that was both confidential and sheepish, "I don't want my husband to know. Not yet."

The girl smiled, charmed by her. "Oh, that's nice," she said. "You're not the first like that. It's such a sweet surprise, I think."

"Me, too," Brenda said.

One of the nice things about this low-impact routine, you could have a quiet conversation under the music because, if you were in any shape at all, what you were doing didn't use up all your breath. The first session, Brenda had taken a position next to a petite blonde in a pink leotard, who turned out to be named June and to be just as gabby as she looked. In two hours and counting, Brenda had learned a lot about June's love life, which tended toward the high impact, but also about this city, this dance studio, and this building.

Which was the point. What Ed did was always illegal and sometimes dangerous, especially when he was teamed with Parker. More than most people, he needed somebody to watch his back. That's what Brenda did, and she'd come in useful more than once. To know the territory was, she believed, part of the job.

And June was happy to talk about the territory. "There wasn't anything like this here before," she explained. "You'd have to go to LA to see a facility like this. Or maybe Vegas."

"Then we're lucky it showed up," Brenda agreed.

"It's all Mrs. Johnson-Ross," June assured her. "She's a local girl, she went away to New York, she had a *career* there, and when this opportunity came along, all this space, she came back and snapped it up."

"Good for her. And good for us."

That conversation had been during lesson number two. Now, in lesson number three, they were both being quiet, following the leader's sinuous movements, Brenda feeling the stretch in those long side muscles it's so hard to tone, and then, in the mirror, she saw the door centered in the wall behind them open and a woman walk in.

Not for a second did Brenda doubt this was Mrs. Johnson-Ross. Tall, too blonde, she carried her just-a-little excess weight as though it were a fashion accessory she was pleased to own. She dressed in verticals, a long dark jacket open over a darker pantsuit with deep lapels, in turn over a blouse in two shades of vertical light blue stripes. The effect was to make the body fade away and emphasize the blonde-framed face, slightly puffy but still very good looking.

Dramatically attractive. How old? Midfifties, maybe.

Brenda turned her head toward June: "There's the boss."

June looked at the mirror, and beamed with pleasure. "Isn't she something?"

"She certainly is."

Mrs. Johnson-Ross, Brenda knew, herself only took individual students, in modern and jazz and ballet, in other smaller rehearsal rooms, leaving the ballroom dancing and aerobics to her staff, though she did occasionally, like now, drop in to see how one of the classes was coming along. Brenda watched her watch the class, then suddenly she realized she was making eye contact.

Mrs. Johnson-Ross did not look away. Expressionless, her blue eyes cold, she looked at Brenda through four beats of the music, as though to memorize her. Then, abruptly, she turned away and, as silently as she'd come in, left the room.

Jesus, she's tough, Brenda thought. I wonder what *that* was all about.

5

The most exciting part of it, Henry Freedman knew, and the thought frightened him as much as it titillated him, was the knowledge that he could be caught at any second, exposed, ruined, as much a pariah as any biblical outcast in his cave. Even more than the sex, it was the danger that aroused Henry. Maybe not the first or second time they'd been together, but every time since.

In the car, driving to or from the assignations, or on the phone, spinning out more tortured lies to Muriel, he kept telling himself he had to stop, he had to stop *now*, the thrill wasn't worth the risk, he wasn't that kind of man. He was fifty-two years of age, for God's sake, he'd never been unfaithful to Muriel in twenty-two years of marriage until the last year and a half. And now he was helpless, he was like a hypnosis subject, it was as though Darlene had a hand inside his trousers and just steadily, inexorably, pulled him toward her.

He'd met Darlene Johnson-Ross more than five years ago, when she'd moved her dance studio into the Armory, the neighbor of his father Jerome, and for nearly four years she'd merely been the attractive if somewhat over-the-hill person he occasionally saw when he visited his father or met with Harrigan, the Armory manager. Henry was one of the more active principals in Armory Associates, the consortium that had bought the old white elephant from the GSA and given it, and the downtown around it, a whole new life. He'd been proud of his part in it, and he'd never for a second suspected that the Armory would be the source of his ruin.

Oh, well, he thought, driving yet again toward the Armory, grin and bear it, though in fact he was doing neither. Tortured, obsessed, so deeply mired in his midlife crisis he couldn't even see it, like a disoriented diver plunging toward the depths while trying desperately to reach the air, Henry drove the Infiniti around the Armory that late afternoon at five-thirty—at least he could still take pride in *that*, the elegance of the conversion—to the garage entrance at the rear, where the massive moatlike gates of the army's time had been removed without a trace.

The garage, one flight down a reinforced ramp, had held obsolete army vehicles for many years, but didn't show it now. At the foot of the ramp, arrowed signs led residential tenants through a locked gate straight ahead, dance studio customers to the left, and Freedman Wholesale Jewels employees—not customers— through an elaborately alarmed gate to the right.

Henry never parked in the dance studio area. As an Armory Associates partner, he had a right to the electronic box on his visor that opened the simple metalpole barrier to residents' parking, which he now used. He left the Infiniti in the visitors' section, rode the elevator up one flight to the main floor, and emerged into the broad low-ceilinged lobby. No one got up to the residential area without being vetted by the doorman.

Who Henry knew very well. "Evening, George," he said, striding across the lobby toward the inner door.

George, in his navy blue uniform with golden piping, had been standing flat-footed, hands behind his back, cap squared off on his head as he gazed out at the street through the glass of the front door, but now he said, "Evening, Mr. Freedman," and moved briskly to his wall-mounted control panel, where he buzzed the inner door open just before Henry arrived, hand already out.

Henry was noted for his "tours of inspection" of the Armory, and saw no reason why anyone would think twice about them. He'd been doing the same thing, though not as often, for years before he'd become besotted with Darlene.

The inner lobby was more spacious, with never-used sofas, all in muted tones of gold and avocado. At the left rear, past the second bank of elevators, was an un-marked gold door to which Henry had the credit-card-style key. Now he inserted it, saw the green light, removed the card, and stepped through into Dar-lene's private office, all stark silver and white, with ac-cents of an icy blue. But it was empty.

Usually, Darlene was here when he entered, not one to tease by being late, to keep him waiting. Usually, she was right here, either elegant in her businesswoman mode or hot and perspiring in leotard from a private lesson, when she would be girlish and giggly and out of breath, crying, "Oh, I'm all sweaty, let me shower, I'm too sweaty!" And he'd say, "I'll lick it off. Come here, let me help, don't wriggle so much."

But today she wasn't here. The office was actually part of a suite, with a small bedroom and bath and kitchenette, but when he went through they were all empty as well.

He got back to the main office just as she came in from the hall, beyond which were the studios. She looked very different, not her normal self at all. She was still beautiful and desirable, today the busi-nesswoman in a long dark jacket and pantsuit and blue striped blouse, but her manner was troubled, almost angry.

"Henry," she said, and her manner was not at all sexy or kittenish, "I'm glad you're here."

What an odd thing to say. "Darlene," he reminded her, "we have a date."

She blinked at him, as though trying to make him out through some sort of fog. "Yes, of course we do," she said. "But it's just— I've come across something, and I don't like it."

Doom! he thought, and his heart contracted like a rubber ball. "Come across something? What?"

"There's a young woman here," Darlene told him, and Henry's heart and body and mind all relaxed. This was just business, that's all, it wasn't exposure. Not yet.

Darlene was saying, "She's in the low-impact class, I wouldn't have noticed her, except she's in better shape than most of them when they start in that class; in fact, they start there *because* they need to get in shape—"

"Darlene," Henry said, ready to be helpful and re-assuring, now that it was merely a business problem, "just tell me what's wrong."

"All right," Darlene said. "Make me a drink."

She usually didn't have her scotch-and-water until after they'd been to bed. He said, "Are you sure?"

"I'm sure," she said, in a tone that asked for no argument.

"Fine, fine." Lifting his hands in amiable surrender, he went over to the credenza behind her desk where the liquor cabinet and glasses and tiny refrigerator were concealed.

While he made her a drink—pointedly, nothing for himself—she said, "I wouldn't have noticed a thing, but Susanna told me—you know, the girl now on the front desk."

"Is that her name?"

"She told me, this new one, Brenda Fawcett, was paying cash because she didn't want her husband to know she was learning to dance. We get some like that from time to time. I don't think it usually turns out to be the happy surprise the lady had in mind."

Henry brought her her drink: "Don't be cynical."

"It's hard not to be." She sighed. "All right. The first thing I thought, if this Brenda Fawcett is here to learn dancing behind her husband's back, why is she in the low-impact class? Why isn't she in ballroom dancing?"

Henry shrugged. "Getting in shape, like you said."

"She's *in* shape." Darlene took a healthy swallow of her drink. "Then I noticed," she said, "our Brenda doesn't wear a wedding ring."

"Some people don't," Henry suggested.

"Some *men* don't," Darlene told him. "Women wear that band."

Marriage discussions with Darlene could be a tricky area. "Fine," Henry said.

"So," Darlene went on, leaving marriage behind, "I looked at the card Susanna filled out, when Ms. Fawcett first enrolled, and it's all false."

Henry frowned at her. "It's what?"

"The home address," Darlene told him, "the phone number, all fake. *And* she's paying in cash, so she doesn't have to prove her identity. So what's she up to?"

Oh, my God, Henry thought, because he *knew*. Private detectives! That's what it was, that's what it *had* to be!

Muriel must have found out—the way he'd been flaunting himself, for God's sake, she *had* to find out—and instead of confronting him, she'd done it this way. Private detectives.

Yes, that was her style, that's how she'd handle it. No discussion, no hope for forgiveness. Just get the evidence, sue for divorce, all open and public and forever damning.

Darlene paced, frowning at the carpet. "All I can think is," she said, "the IRS. Or more likely the state tax people. *That's* why she's paying cash, trying to trap us, see what we do with unrecorded income."

I can't tell her the truth, Henry realized. I should pack a suitcase, keep it in the trunk of the car. In case . . . Whenever . . .

"The little *bitch!*" Darlene raged. "Henry, am I right? What else could it be?"

"You'll just have to—" Henry began and coughed, and tried again: "You'll just have to keep an eye on her. I believe I'll—I believe I'll have a drink now, too."

"No, wait," she said, surprising him.

He paused, halfway to the drinks cabinet. "Why not?"

"That class is almost over," she told him. "Go get your car, bring it around front. We'll follow her. We'll *see* if she doesn't wind up in the State Office Building."

Or the private detective's office, Henry thought. Much more likely, the private detective's office.

But wouldn't it be better to know the worst, *know* it and be able to decide what to do?

Looking around the office, eying the open bedroom door, he said, "Our lovely afternoon."

"We'll still have it, Henry," she promised him. "We'll follow her, we'll find *out* what she's up to, and then we'll come right back here. Henry . . ."

He looked at her. "Yes?"

He loved that lascivious smile she sometimes showed; not often enough. "It'll be better than ever," she whispered.

On the way back to the Infiniti, he thought, I'll have to phone Muriel, I'm going to be later than I thought. I'll have to phone her, I'll have to tell her . . . whatever I tell her.

6

When CID Detective Jason Rembek, a big shambling balding man with thick eyeglasses sliding down his lumpy nose, reached his cubicle at Headquarters at 8:34 Saturday morning—according to the digital clock on his desk, which was never wrong—the overnights were stacked waiting for him, escape-related materials on top, lesser cases underneath, just as he'd instructed.

The flight of the three hardcases from Stoneveldt Thursday afternoon had kept him on the hop all day yesterday. He hoped things would be quieter today. He had other Opens on his desk, not just these three punks taking a little vacation.

Detective Rembek had been on the state force fourteen years, with very little experience of prison breaks. None, from Stoneveldt; that trio had made the record books. Nevertheless, it was his own experience and the experience of others he'd talked to or read about, that the boys in prison were mostly there in the first place because they didn't know how to handle life on the outside, not even when they *weren't* on the run. Very very rare was the guy who disappeared forever, or showed up thirty years later a solid citizen, mayor of some small town in Canada.

Mostly, the escapees ran until they got tired and then just stood there until they were rounded up. Sometimes they'd steal a car or rob a convenience store, but there was no *plan* in their lives, no long-term goal. Three, four days, they'd start to get hungry, they'd start to miss that regular life they had in the cells, and they'd call it quits. Detective Rembek believed it was true almost without exception that once an escapee had thought about *escape*, he was finished thinking.

Were these three going to fit the pattern? Why not? On Rembek's desk were photos and bios of the three, and there was little in them to make him believe they were going to beat the odds. The two local boys, anyway. Given their histories, their family ties, their dependency on this small area of the world, it was only a matter of time before they'd show up somewhere they'd been before, that they just couldn't stay away from. A relative, a girlfriend, a bar, a fellow heister. And then the net would scoop them up, put them back where they belonged.

The out-of-towner was the wild card; Ronald Kasper, or whatever his name was. No one had ever escaped from Stoneveldt, but these three had, and neither

Marcantoni nor Williams seemed to Rembek the kind
of guy to break that cherry. So was Kasper the one
who'd made it happen? Was he the one they had to
find, the one they had to outthink and outguess, if
they were going to collect all three?

Rembek studied the few pictures he had of Kasper.
A hard face, bony, like outcroppings of stone. Hard
eyes; if they were the windows of the soul, the shades
were drawn.

Rembek didn't pick up any of the pictures, but
leaned closer and closer over them, his nose almost
touching the surface of the desk. Had this bird gone
through plastic surgery some time in the past? Did he
have other histories, beyond the broken burglary at
the warehouse and the escape from Stoneveldt? Rembek craved the opportunity to interrogate that face,
see what was behind those eyes.

Well. There were other ways to come at them. The
three escapees now on his desk had three contact
points, being the people who had visited them during
their time inside; one each. Ronald Kasper had been
visited several times by his brother-in-law, named Ed
Mackey. Thomas Marcantoni had been visited twice by
his brother, Angelo. And Brandon Williams had been
visited three times by his youngest sister, Maryenne.

The first of these was the most interesting. After
Kasper broke out, police naturally went to the motel
where Mackey was living, only to learn he'd checked
out that morning, no forwarding address, no useful

ID. Detective Rembek doubted very much it was a coincidence that Mackey checked out of his motel in the morning on the same day that Kasper checked out of prison in the afternoon.

The top report on Detective Rembek's desk told him that no progress had been made in either finding Mackey or learning who he actually was. The next two folders were mostly the results of the wiretaps on Angelo Marcantoni and Maryenne Williams, wiretaps that had been granted by the judge at nine P.M. on Thursday, less than four hours after the escape, and had been in operation ever since. No police officer actually sat next to the recording machine twenty-four hours a day; it was a voice-activated tape, picked up at eight every morning, and four in the afternoon, and midnight.

Angelo Marcantoni, according to the transcript, did very little on the telephone, and then it seemed to be mostly about bowling; if that were a code, as far as Detective Rembek was concerned, Marcantoni was welcome to it. In any event, he appeared to be the law-abiding brother, married, three children, with absolutely no criminal record of any kind and an unblemished work record with a supermarket chain. Detective Rembek thought it unlikely he would risk all that to help a brother who'd been in increasingly serious trouble since he was ten.

As for Maryenne Williams, she appeared to be a young mother who spent all her waking hours on the phone with other young mothers, discussing their babies, discussing their babies' (mostly absent) fathers, and discussing boys they thought of as "cute"; as though they didn't have trouble enough already. That's what the MW transcripts had been up till now, and that's what they looked like for last night, too, boring and tedious to read but necessary.

And then:

11:19 P.M.

MW: Hello?

C: Hi, it's me.

MW: (audible gasp) Are you okay?

Detective Rembek sat straighter, holding in both hands the paper he was reading.

C: Yeah, I'm fine.

MW: What are you gonna do?

C: I think I gotta go away.

MW: Oh, yeah, you do. You need money?

C: I'm gonna get money in a couple days, I'm okay. I got a good place to stay, and next week I'll take off.

MW: Listen, uh—

Almost said his name there, Detective Rembek thought.

MW: —you remember Goody?

C: Yeah, that one.

MW: Well, he come around, he said, any way he can help, buy you tickets or stuff, whatever, you should call him, because it wouldn't be good for me to do anything.

C: No, no, you shouldn't do anything. I'm just calling— I wanted to tell you I'm okay, and I'll be going away, next week.

MW: That's the best thing. If you need help—

C: Goody.

I wish I could hear how he said that name, Detective Rembek thought. Does he think Goody will help him, or does he think Goody isn't any use? He won't tell his sister, because she thinks this Goody is all right.

MW: I'm glad you called.

C: Well, yeah, I had to. Listen, kiss Vernon for me.

MW: I will. (crying) Bye, now.

C: Bye, now.

The call had been traced, after the event, to a payphone on Russell Street, a nondescript working-class neighborhood. Two police officers were at this moment searching the area, with no realistic expectation of finding anything.

Detective Rembek took notes. Goody; find this fellow Goody, squeeze him a little, see where he leads.

And there was one other thing. Detective Rembek looked back through the transcript and found it:

C: I'm gonna get money in a couple days, I'm okay.

Going to get money in a couple days. Where?

7

It took Buck two days to figure it out. He'd known from the get-go there was something funny going on with that little scumbag Goody, to make him all of a sudden up and leave his sales post early on a Thursday, but he just couldn't see in his mind what Goody was up to. A family emergency; shit. What would a piece of garbage like Goody be doing with a family?

But if it was something else that took Goody away in the middle of the best sales period of the day, when the workingman wanted a little taste to bring home with him after another eight hours throwing his life away for pennies to the Man, what was it? I'm not stupid, Buck reminded himself. If there's something there, and there's got to be something there, what the hell is it?

Of course he saw all the stuff on the television Thursday night about the three boys broke out of Stoneveldt prison, and he even noticed that one of them was a brother, but he never made the connection. And he didn't make that connection because he didn't think about the police scanner in brother Goody's car until Goody forgot and left it on that Saturday evening when he swung by the Land Rover to turn in the day's cash and stash. With both windows open, Buck's Land Rover and Goody's Mercury, all of a sudden there was that harsh cop-radio voice, *jabber-jabber-jabber*, until Goody quickly reached down and switched it off. And even then Buck didn't put two and two together, because he was distracted by business, there being three more salesmen to report in, and it wasn't until he was dealing with the second of those that he suddenly saw the light.

The brother's on the run. Big-time manhunt, all the cops excited because these three guys rubbed their nose in it, escaped from their im-*preg*-nable slammer, and Buck knew what that meant. And he knew that Goody would instantly know what that meant, too.

Reward.

He's got a connection to the brother, Buck told himself. He's looking to collect; turn the boy in and collect, without telling his best friend—and employer, don't forget—Buck.

"Leon," he said to the bodyguard in the passenger seat up front, "call my mama, tell her bring the Lincoln up, leave it out front. Raydiford," he said to the bodyguard at the wheel, "as soon as Hector check in,

you drop Leon and me at the Lincoln, then take Rover
and all this shit to the store."

Leon looked happy. "We goin somewhere?"

"We're goin callin," Buck told him.

One thing you could say for Goody; he didn't put
all his profits in his nose. A lot of them, they could
only function at all because they were too scared of
Buck to allow themselves to fuck up totally, but Goody
had a brain and knew how to stay on plan.

Look at his house. An actual real house, not some
rathole apartment in the very slums you're dealing so
you can get out of. Not as good a place, of course, as
Buck's horse ranch out in the country, but for a street
dealer not bad; a big sprawling brick home with a wide
porch on the front and sides, late nineteenth century,
set on a wide lawn amid similar houses in a residential
section that had been a suburb when the doctors and
the college professors first built their places out here.
That had been before cars, so some of these places still
didn't have garages, just driveways, including Goody's,
and there was his Mercury now, parked beside his
house. Goody was home.

A telephone company truck was in front of the
house, a lineman in a cherry picker doing something
at the top of the pole, so Leon had to drive beyond it
and pull the Lincoln in at the curb in front of the
house next door. Buck, spread out in back, waited
while Leon came trotting around to open his door,

and then the two of them went up to Goody's house, stepped up onto the wide wood-floored porch, and Leon rang the doorbell.

They had to wait a pretty long time, and Buck was just about to tell Leon to bust the door in, when it opened, and there stood a white girl, college girl, in blue jeans and white tank top, coked to the eyebrows. She frowned through her personal mist at Buck and Leon and said, "Yes? What can I do for you?"

"Not a thing," Buck said, and brushed by her.

She tottered, very shaky, but didn't fall down because she still had a good hold of the doorknob. "Hey!" she cried, but her outrage was unfocused, and she didn't seem to notice when Leon copped a feel on the way by.

You can take the boy out of the pisshole, but you can't take the pisshole out of the boy. There was barely any furniture at all in these big echoing rooms with the good old wood floors. In the front room, a television set with its other machines sat on an assemble-it-yourself bookcase from the home center, full of tapes and DVDs. Two big white wicker chairs with peacock-tail backs stood across the room, facing the TV, with a couple of mismatched shitty little tables, table lamps standing on the floor, telephone on the floor.

Pool table in the next room, what would have been the dining room, with two scruffy backless couches along one wall. And here came Goody, out of what must be the kitchen, a beer bottle in one hand, cigar in the other.

He came out of there full of swagger, a tough guy, wanting to know what the commotion was at his front door, but when he saw Buck he stumbled, next to the pool table, and got scared. He didn't know yet what the problem was, but if Buck himself was all of a sudden in Goody's house, Goody knew it was time to get scared.

"Hey, Buck," he said. "You didn't tell me you were comin over, man."

"I was in the neighborhood," Buck told him, but he didn't bother to smile. He said, "You been in touch with Brandon Williams yet?"

Surprise, and being scared, made Goody stupid. He said, "Who?"

Now Buck did smile, in a not-friendly way. "Think of that, Leon," he said. "This fool here's the only man, woman, or child in this city never heard of Brandon Williams."

"Oh, Brandon *Williams!*" Goody cried, acting out all kinds of sudden recognition. "I didn't connect the name, you know, all of a sudden like that."

"Leon," Buck said, "go hit that fool, like he was a TV wouldn't come into focus."

"No, wait, Buck—Aa!"

Buck looked at him, leaning against the wall. In the front room, the college girl had sat in one of the peacock wicker chairs and was gazing at the television set, which was turned off. Buck said, "You in focus now, fool?"

"Just tell me, Buck," Goody begged him. The beer

bottle and cigar were both at his feet, but he paid them no attention. "All you gotta do is tell me," he said. "You know I come through for you."

Buck said, "Tell me about your family emergency, Thursday."

A whole lot of lies hovered just inside Goody's trembling lips, Buck could see their meaty wings in there, but finally Goody wasn't that big a fool, and what he said was, "The police scanner. I heard it on the scanner."

"Brandon Williams is outa the box."

"His sister, his little sister, Maryenne, she's an old friend of mine, Buck. A *good* girl, I like her, not like this white trash here, I thought, I gotta go be there when she finds out, I gotta tell her myself, so it won't be that big of a, you know, a shock."

"Reward money," Buck said.

"Aw, no, Buck," Goody said, because he was still to some extent a fool, "I wanna help that girl, old-friend like—"

"Leon," Buck said, "He's losin his focus."

"No, Buck, I—Aaoww! Listen, don't—Ohh! *Owww!*"

"Okay, Leon," Buck said, "let's see is he tuned in."

"Jesus, Buck, he's gonna break somethin on me, don't do this, man."

"Tell me your story, Goody."

Goody looked at the beer bottle at his feet. Most of the beer had spilled onto the floor, but a little was left in the bottle, visible through the green glass. Goody licked his lips. "Uhh," he said. He met Buck's eyes, wincing, and nodded, and said, "I called her, on the cell. Her cell, from my cell. When I heard on the scanner. I went over there, you know, her place, told her, she can't help her brother, cops be all over her, watchin, see what she—"

"Move it along, Goody," Buck said.

Goody nodded, quickly. "She says okay," he said. "We both know he's gonna call her, she's gonna tell him, call good old Goody, he'll help out, get you airplane tickets, whatever."

Buck said, "When did he call?"

"He didn't yet," Goody said, then looked wide-eyed at Leon, then back at Buck: "Honest to God! I figured, tomorrow morning, I'd go over there, see Maryenne again, after her and her family get outa church."

"Churchgoing people," Buck said.

"I told you," Goody said, "she's a good girl, she's okay, I wanna help out, I really do, Buck."

"You want that reward," Buck said.

Goody spread his hands. "What reward? I didn't see nothing about no reward. If you know about—"

"Leon."

"Buck, no! Aii! Ow! Oh, *no!* All right, Buck, I—Ow! *Gee*-ziz! I *said* all right! Ow! Stop! Ow!"

"All right, Leon," Buck said. To Goody he said, "It's when *I* say all right that Leon hears it."

"Ohhh. I can't stand up no more, Buck."

"We could nail you to the wall, you like."

"Buck, please."

"This Brandon Williams," Buck said, "he's gonna call his sister. Then he's gonna call you. Right?"

"That's the plan. That's the plan, Buck."

"*When* he calls you," Buck said, "the second thing you're gonna do is call the police, start the negotiation. What's the first thing you're gonna do, Goody?"

"I'm gonna call you," Goody said. He was very subdued now. He didn't like the situation, but he knew he was defeated. He was also in pain.

"That's right," Buck said. "You call me first, then you can go on and do the negotiation with the law, same as you planned. You'll collect the reward, same as you already figured."

Trying to look hopeful, Goody said, "And we split it, right?"

"We'll work that out, Goody," Buck said. "Okay, Leon, we're done here."

They left Goody huddled against the wall. Going through the front room, Buck nodded at the college girl and said, "You oughta wring that out before you put it back where you found it."

"That's what I planned on, Buck," Goody said. His voice was high, with a new tremble in it. "But now," he said, "I think I just gotta rest awhile."

Outside, the telephone company truck was gone. Some other emergency taken care of, working this late on a Saturday night.

8

Hold on, Brenda," Ed Mackey said. He held tight to her hips, felt her knees press to both sides of his rib cage, and looked up at her grinning grimace as she concentrated on that inner rhythm, bore down, eyes staring at some point inside her own head. "Hold on, Brenda, hold on."

"You know," she muttered, "you know, you know, come *along* with me, you know, you know—"

"Hold on—"

"Come *along* with me!"

"Hold oonnn!"

He thrust endlessly upward, back arched, and she shivered all over like a bead curtain. "Oh!" she cried. "*You* know!"

The shower stall, when they got to it five minutes later, was big enough for them both. This was one of the most expensive top-floor rooms in one of the most expensive hotels in the city, and Brenda had been checked in here for five days now, ever since Parker had told Mackey when he and the other two would be coming out of Stoneveldt. Mackey had kept the old motel room for himself until Thursday, and was not registered in this hotel, was merely a visitor, because he'd known, once Parker was out, the law would want to have a word or two with the guy who'd been coming to see Parker inside.

So Brenda was here to give him somewhere else to wait out the jewelry job, and she was *here* because Mackey believed, when the cops were looking for somebody, they looked first in places at the same economic level where they'd known the guy to live before. So let them spend a week on cut-rate motels; by the time they thought to look at someplace like the Park Regal, Mackey and Brenda would be long gone from here.

Out of the shower, Mackey dressed in dark, loose comfortable clothes, with a Beretta Jaguar .22 automatic in a deerskin holster at the small of his back, under his shirt, upside down with the butt to the right, ready to his hand if he had to reach back there. He'd gotten similar gear for Parker and Williams. Rubber gloves and a small tube of talcum powder were in his jacket pocket. He packed a small canvas bag with a few of his things, because he'd be staying with the rest of them at the former beer distributor's place between the job and the arrival of the fence from New Orleans. Then he'd phone Brenda, she'd pick him up, and they'd be off. With Parker, if he wanted a ride, or on their own.

He kissed her at the door, and she said, "Try to stay out of trouble."

"What you should do," he told her, "is stay away from that armory. Don't call attention." Because he knew she liked to be nearby when he was at work, in case he needed her. He'd needed her in the past, but not this time. "Just stay away, Brenda," he said. "Okay?"

"I'll go over there tomorrow," she told him, "for one more class at the dance studio. I like that workout. I won't go today, there's nobody there today, everything's closed on Sunday."

"We know," Mackey said, and grinned, kissed her again, and left.

Downstairs, Phil Kolaski was supposed to be waiting for him in the Honda, down the block from the hotel entrance, and there he was. Mackey tossed his bag in back, got into the passenger seat in front, and said, "Everything still on?"

"Don't see why not," Phil said, and drove them away from there.

It was Phil Kolaski that Mackey had gotten in touch with, when he was the outside man to help Parker put together a string on the inside. They had studied each other very closely, looking for danger signs, and had both decided they could take a chance.

It was like a marriage, that, or more exactly like an engagement. The two people start off strangers to each other, have to find reasons to trust each other, have to learn each other well enough to feel they aren't likely to be betrayed, and then have to pop the question:

"Tom's got a job lined up for when he gets out. He'll want you and your friend in on it, to take the place of the guys got nabbed with him."

Mackey had been comfortable with that idea—if he was in this part of the world anyway, he might as well make a profit on it—but knew that Parker would want, once out, to keep moving. He'd told Phil that, and Phil had said, "Tom will talk to him, before they come out," so it seemed to be all right.

Two blocks from the Park Regal they went through the intersection with the Armory on the left and the library, another heavy brick pile from the nineteenth century, on the right. Mackey laughed: "We're gonna be *under* this street!"

"With our hands," Phil said, "full of jewels."

9

The Margaret H. Moran Memorial Library was theoretically closed as of five P.M. on Sundays, but by the time the last patron and the last book/tape/DVD were checked out it was usually closer to five-thirty. Then whichever staff was on duty had to go through the public parts of the building for strays, occasionally finding one (usually in a lavatory), so that they were lucky if they were out of there, front door locked behind them and alarms switched on, by quarter to six.

This evening, late October twilight coming on fast, the library was dark and empty at six P.M., when a black Honda and a green Taurus drove slowly by. The two cars traveled on another block to a parking garage where they entered, took checks from the automatic machine at the entrance, left the cars, walked back down the concrete stairwell to the street, and separated. Parker and Mackey turned left, away from the library and Armory, while Williams crossed Indiana

Avenue and Marcantoni and Kolaski and Angioni walked back to the library.

At the library, Marcantoni hunkered in front of the door while the other two stood on the sidewalk in front of him, chatting together, blocking the view of Marcantoni at work from passing cars. There was little traffic and no pedestrians in this downtown area at six on a Sunday.

Marcantoni opened a flat soft leather pouch on his knee; inside, in a row of narrow pockets, were his picks. Patiently he went to work on the locks, not wanting to disturb them so much as to set off the building's alarms.

The fire law required the door to open outward. Marcantoni pulled it ajar just enough so he could put a small matchbox in the opening, to keep the spring lock from shutting it again. Then he put his picks neatly away, and was straightening when Parker and Mackey approached, with Williams behind them, just coming around the corner.

The six men went into the building, closing the re-locked door behind them. Marcantoni said, "There's wastebaskets behind the main counter there, we're gonna need them. There's a lot of trash to move."

Parker said, "Then you need shovels."

"Right," Marcantoni said. "I've got that figured out, too."

There were three large metal wastebaskets, gray, square, behind the long main counter, all having been emptied by the staff before they left. Kolaski stacked the three and carried them, and Marcantoni, the only one who knew the route, led the way down the center aisle, book stacks on both sides. He carried a small flashlight, with electric tape blocking part of the lens, and Angioni carried a similar one, coming last. They picked up two more wastebaskets from desks along the way, these carried by Williams.

Toward the rear of the main section Marcantoni turned left to go down a broad flight of stairs that doubled back at a landing. This led them down to the periodicals section, with its own stacks full of bound magazines and its own reading room lined with long oak tables. "We'll come back for a couple of those," Marcantoni said, waving the flashlight beam over the tables as they walked toward the rear of the section.

Back here was another counter, for checking out magazines and microfilm. They picked up two more wastebaskets there, plus something else. "Look at this," Marcantoni said.

On a separate wheeled metal table behind the counter were stacked several rows of small metal file drawers. Marcantoni opened one, pulled the full drawer out completely, and dumped the cards onto the floor. Shining the flashlight into the empty drawer, sixteen inches long, six inches wide, four inches deep, he said, "A shovel. Everybody grab one."

They did, and moved on. In the rear wall, next to a coin-slot copying machine, was a broad wooden door marked NO ADMITTANCE. Marcantoni handed his flashlight to Williams, then got down to one knee and brought out his picks. "This one's nothing," he said.

Angioni and Williams shone light on the lock, Marcantoni worked with smooth speed, and he pushed the door open in just under a minute. The others waited while he put his picks away and stood, then Williams gave him back the flashlight. Carrying the wastebaskets and file drawers, they entered a storage area lined with rows of metal shelving.

"There's no windows down here," Marcantoni said. He closed the door they'd just come through, then hit the switch beside it. Fluorescent ceiling fixtures lit up to show a deep but narrow room with the metal shelves on both sides and across the back. "It's down there," Marcantoni said, and led the way to the rear, where the shelves were stacked with copier supplies.

Even with all the light on it, the door was hard to see, through the shelves stacked with boxes and rolls. It was painted the same neutral gray as the wall and the metal shelving.

Marcantoni said, "These shelves aren't fixed to the wall. I just pulled one end out, the other time."

There was not much clearance between the rear and side shelving. Williams tugged on the shelving's left end and its legs made a shrieking noise on the floor, so he lifted the end instead. Mackey went over to help, and they wheeled the shelving out till it faced up against the right-side shelves.

Angioni was studying the door, featureless metal

with barely visible hinges on the right side. In its middle, at about waist height, was a round hole less than an inch in diameter. Angioni said, "That's the keyhole?"

"That's it," Marcantoni said. Walking over to the door, he took from his pockets a small socket wrench and a star-shaped bit. As he fitted them together at right angles, he said, "The last time, I didn't want to mess up this door so somebody might notice something. I looked at the lock on the door at the other end, and I figured this one would be the same. It's a double bar that extends beyond the door to both sides, hinged in the middle so it'll pivot to unlock it. This works."

Bending to the door, he inserted the bit into the hole, with the wrench extended to the right. With both hands on the wrench, he lifted. The wrench barely moved upward, and from beyond the door they could hear the scrape of metal on metal. "It's goddam stiff," Marcantoni said, "but I got it last— Here it comes."

Slowly he pulled the wrench upward until it was vertical above the hole. "That should do it."

He pulled the bit out, separated the wrench into its two components, and put them away in his pocket, bringing out a short flat-head screwdriver instead. Going down to one knee, he said, "Here's where I pulled it out before. I figured nobody'd notice."

Down close to the floor, where the bottom shelf would have covered it, the edge of the door and its wooden frame showed scratches. Marcantoni forced the screwdriver in there, levered it, and all at once the door popped an inch inward. He got to his feet, putting the screwdriver away. "There," he said. "From now on, it's easy."

To show that, he put the fingers of both hands onto the protruding edge of the door and tugged. More metal-on-metal complaint, and then the door grudgingly came open. The old hinges didn't want to move, but Marcantoni insisted, and at last the door was wide open, angled back away from the entrance.

Now they could look through into the tunnel, illuminated for the first several feet by the fluorescents in the storage room. It was narrow, about the width of an automobile, with brick floor and brick walls up to an arched brick ceiling. Angioni shone his flashlight, but it didn't show much more than the fluorescents did. "It's angled down," he said.

"Yeah," Marcantoni agreed, "it slopes down, not steep, then levels out, then slopes up again on the other side."

"Well," Angioni said, "shall we go?"

"That's why we're here," Mackey pointed out.

Marcantoni said, "Let me get the tape off this flash." He and Angioni peeled the electric tape from the flashlight lenses, and then they started into the tunnel, moving in loose single file, carrying the wastebaskets and the file drawers.

Had the tunnel ever been used? If so, the people who'd been in here left no marks. At the time this had been built, gaslight was common in this part of the world, but it hadn't been installed in here. If someone had been in the tunnel, using some kind of torch for light, there might be smoke smudges on the curved ceiling, but none appeared. It looked as though the tunnel had been built simply because that was the way the plans had been laid out, then it was locked and forgotten.

They walked down the easy slope, the tunnel absolutely straight, then headed along the level section. There was no sound but the brush of their feet. The air was cool and dry, with a faint mustiness. Every twenty feet or so there was a large iron ring jutting from the right side wall at about shoulder level. For sconces? For a guide rope, to be followed in the dark? There was no way to tell.

"There it is," Marcantoni said, and they all came up to cluster at the beginning of the collapse. Just ahead of them, the ceiling had started to fall, three bricks wide at the peak to begin with, then wider. On the floor were the bricks, some broken, and a little debris. Farther on, the two flashlights showed that the collapse had become wider, with a combination of dirt and stone fallen from the hole. By twenty feet from the beginning of the rupture, the debris made a steep mountain slope that completely blocked the tunnel, top to bottom and side to side.

Marcantoni said, "My idea is, the bricks we can push against the side walls, and the rest of it we scoop into the wastebaskets, carry it back a ways, dump it out, leave room to get by."

Williams said, "What if more comes down, when we start moving this shit?"

"It's an old fall," Marcantoni said. "Whatever happened was a long time ago. It's stable now."

Parker said, "When we start to move it, it won't be stable any more."

"Well," Marcantoni said, "this is the route. This is the only way in. And we're here."

They took turns with the flashlights, looking up at the early part of the rupture. The remaining bricks to both sides were solid, hadn't been loosened at all by whatever had happened to the part that fell. Here in its narrowest section, there was shallow emptiness just above where the bricks had been, and then compacted earth. Farther on, more dirt and stone had fallen from above the displaced bricks, so maybe Marcantoni's idea was right, that this was an accident done by the crew removing trolley tracks half a century ago, who never knew they'd done it.

Finally, Mackey said, "I think we can try it, anyway. If more of it starts to fall in, though, I've got to tell you, I'm going back to the library, and anyone who wants my share can have it."

"Listen, we can do it," Angioni said. "Come on, Tom. A couple you guys go get tables."

Williams and Mackey went away, pleased to go, taking one of the flashlights. Parker held the other, and the remaining three moved slowly forward, at first kicking bricks and debris to the side, and then, when it got to be more than that, scooping the file drawers into the slope of the debris mountain, dumping dirt and stones into the wastebaskets. They stacked bricks to the sides, and carried heavy baskets back along the tunnel to empty into little pyramids of trash. From time to time, the slope ahead of them made small shifts, and they could hear stones pattering down its side, but then it would be silent again.

By the time Mackey and Williams had made three round-trips, bringing one of the eight-foot-long tables back with them each time, lining the tables up in a long row, the other four had progressed into the trash mountain, which was loose and easily disassembled. Parker had spelled Kiloski, and then Kiloski had given the flashlight to Angioni, and now Marcantoni had it.

Above them, they were now at the serious part of the rupture, where the tear in the ceiling was a dozen bricks wide and where, when the flashlight beam was aimed up there, it was all a dark emptiness, like a vertical cavern. But nothing else seemed to want to come down out of there, so they kept working, and now Mackey and Williams joined them, and from that point on three cleared debris while two carried the full wastebaskets back to empty, and one held both flashlights.

They worked for more than three hours, from time to time sliding the tables forward. They didn't try to clear all the trash out of the way, just enough so they could keep moving forward and bringing the tables along after them.

Finally, Marcantoni said, "Listen!"

They all listened, and heard the faint sound, the rustle of dirt sliding down a slope, and Angioni said, "Is that the other side?"

"You know it is," Marcantoni told him. "We're almost through."

Still it took another half hour to finish this part of it. When they moved the tables forward now, the easiest way was to go on all fours underneath and juke them along that way. Soon they could start emptying the wastebaskets into the cleared area ahead, which made things go faster.

And it looked as though Marcantoni's estimate of the length of the collapse was right. The length of the three tables would total just a little longer distance than the rupture above them. Nothing additional fell while they worked, but the tables gave them a sense there'd still be a way out if things went bad.

Williams had the flashlights when they first broke through. "Hey, wait," he said. "I can see it. Tom, there's your damn door."

They were looking through an ellipsis, less than a foot wide, brick and rupture above, rubble below, at a dark continuation of the tunnel. At the far end, just picking up the gleam from the flashlights, was the black iron door.

At this end, the rupture in the ceiling had narrowed again, with less debris having fallen down. They moved more quickly, wanting to get this part over with, and then Marcantoni strode on ahead, not bothering about a flashlight. When he reached the door, he had his wrench-and-bit assembled, and with one move he had the door unlocked; one kick, and it was open.

A dry breeze whispered through the tunnel, maybe for the first time. A few pebbles rattled onto the tables.

On the far side, the iron door led to a nearly empty storage room, thick with dust. A few old glass display cases had been shoved haphazardly against the side wall, along with an upright metal locker with a broken hinge, a jeweler's suitcase with a broken wheel, and other things that should have been thrown away. Whatever the army had used this space for, if anything, Freedman Wholesale Jewel used it, when they remembered it at all, as a garbage dump.

Crossing this room to the door in the opposite wall, Marcantoni said, "I was only here during the rehab, so I don't know the layout now. I only know the plans didn't have a lot of interior alarms, because they counted on the building to take care of that." He tried the knob and cursed. "What the hell'd they lock it for?"

Kolaski said, "That's a rare antique suitcase."

"Shit," Marcantoni said. "Gimme a minute."

It didn't take much more, and then they moved on into a broad dimly lit area; the employees' parking lot under the main store, empty on a Sunday night. Exit lights and a few fire-code lights led them diagonally across the big concrete-floored room with its white lines defining parking spaces to where an illuminated sign, white letters on green, read STAIRS.

The stairs were also concrete, with a landing at the top and a closed firedoor that was also locked. "Shit," Marcantoni said, and reached for his tools.

Parker said, "That door is going to be alarmed."

Angioni said, "Why? I thought the whole idea was, these people don't give a shit about security because they've got this whole armory around them."

Mackey said, "No, Parker's right."

"Damn it," Marcantoni said, "this is the only way in. This, and the front door. Front door for customers, this door for employees that park their cars downstairs. No other way in."

Williams said, "This is also gonna be a firewall. Concrete block. So we don't bypass the alarm by going through the wall."

Marcantoni said, "We come this far. Now what?"

"We go in," Parker said.

Marcantoni gave him a surprised look. "But you just said it's alarmed."

"It'll be just this door," Parker told him. "There isn't any reason to link it with the entrance up at the front, so it isn't part of a whole system, there's nothing else to hook up to it."

Marcantoni nodded. "That sounds right."

Parker said, "Since it's just this one door, there'll be a keypad on the inside, and we'll have thirty seconds, maybe forty-five seconds, to short-circuit it."

Kolaski said, "I'm very good at that, that's a specialty of mine."

"It's yours," Marcantoni told him.

Parker said, "What it means is, he's got to be able to get in there fast. Once you start playing with it, the countdown starts."

Marcantoni gave the door lock a look of contempt. "This? A sneeze and it's open."

"Then go sneeze, Tom," Kolaski said, taking out his own canvas pouch of tools, saying to Angioni, "Hold this open for me, will you?"

Marcantoni looked around to see that everybody was in agreement and ready, then bent over the lock. He worked with concentration and speed, then pushed the door open, stepped back, and said, "Go, Phil."

Kolaski stepped through the doorway, followed by Angioni holding up the opened tool pouch. A small pale keypad was mounted on the wall to the left of the door, near the lock. Four Phillips-head screws held it in place. Kolaski chose a tool, spun the screws loose, chose a tool, popped the top of the keypad cover loose so that it flopped forward and down to hang from its wires, chose tiny alligator clips, put them on the connectors at the back of the keypad, stepped back, said, "Done."

Angioni laughed as Kolaski put his tool pouch away. "I love a showboat," he said.

"It's just talent," Kolaski assured him.

They stepped through into a space that wasn't entirely dark, since it was spotted with red exit signs, one over the door they'd just come through. They were at a T intersection of hallways, one going left and right, the other straight ahead, exit signs over the doors at the far ends. Closed or open doors were spaced along the halls.

Angioni said, "This doesn't look like a jeweler."

"It isn't," Kolaski told him, "it's a wholesaler. It's more about offices and salesmen, not display."

Parker said, "What we want will be toward the front."

They walked down the hall ahead of them, seeing ordinary offices through the open doorways they passed. The door at the end of the hall swung inward, and when they opened it they read on its other side NO ADMITTANCE. That made Kolaski laugh: "Comin *outa* the No Admittance, that's somethin new."

Directly in front of them, beyond the No Admittance door, were three large messy desks mounted with computers and phones and reference books and stacks of sales and tax forms, flanked by extra chairs. These desks faced outward, away from them, toward a broad sales or display floor, where display cases mingled with smaller desks and cashier stations. Globe lights hung low all around the room from a high metal gridwork; these were all switched off, but lights gleamed within display cases here and there, enough to dimly illuminate the room.

Angioni, grinning at it all, said, "This is the place, all right."

Williams said, "Does the doorman out front get to see in here?"

"No," Marcantoni told him, "there's a solid metal door comes down over the entrance at night."

"So it's all ours," Kolaski said, "so let's get to it."

They all had rubber or plastic gloves, which they now pulled on. Before this, Marcantoni had done most of the touching, except for when the tables were moved, and he and the others had wiped prints away as they went, but from now on that wouldn't be possible. They all pulled supermarket plastic bags from their pockets, two each, and started moving through the display area, picking whatever attracted their eyes.

The displays were different from those in a retail store. They gave as much space to manufacturers' brochures and specifications as they did to the items being offered for sale. Two or three of the cases contained only different kinds of small gift boxes for jewelry, and one other presented a great variety of clasps and hooks and pins.

But most of the cases contained value. Wedding and engagement rings; bracelets, necklaces, brooches; gold money clips shaped like dollar signs, pound signs, euro signs; watches that would cost retail as much as a midsize car.

The six moved among it all like the gleaners who come through the field after the main harvest, picking and choosing only the best of what was on offer, breaking the glass that was the final barrier in their way. It had taken them more than three hours to get in here, but only twenty minutes before all twelve bags were full, looped to their belts so their hands were still free.

"A good night," Marcantoni said, and grinned at Parker. "I told you you'd like to stick around."

"You told me," Parker said.

Going back, they paused while Kolaski reclaimed his alligator clips, replacing them, now that he had the leisure for it, with a simpler wire connection. Then they moved on, letting that spring-mounted door close behind them as they trotted down the stairs to the parking garage, across the broad concrete floor tinged green from the stairs sign behind them, through the nearly empty storage room, and back into the tunnel.

Now they needed the flashlights again. Marcantoni still had his, and Mackey now had the other. They shone the lights ahead, and the air floated with dust, like mist over a swamp.

"Now what?" Marcantoni said.

They walked forward into the tunnel, smelling the dry chalky dust, feeling the grit of it in their noses and mouths. Ahead, the mountain of rubble was back.

They stopped to look at it. Maybe the vibration of their passage had done it, or just the new movement of air from both doors being open at the ends of the tunnel, but something had caused a further fall from above the ceiling. Some bricks had come down, but mostly it was dirt and stone, loose but compacting. It covered the tables, except for a narrow bit at this end. Above, it sloped up and away to where the ceiling used to be and farther.

"All I hope," Mackey said, "is we don't wind up with some delivery truck down here with us. This is under the street."

"We're too far down," Marcantoni told him. "Besides, we're not gonna stay." He was on one knee again, bending down, shining the flashlight under the end of table that jutted out from the fresh fall of debris. "I can see all the way through," he said. "These things did their job."

"They damn well better," Angioni said. "We got no other way outa here."

"I'll go first with the light," Marcantoni said, and on elbows and knees started through the tunnel-within-a-tunnel created by the tables.

"I'm with you," Angioni said, and went down on all fours to crawl after him.

Marcantoni was the biggest of the six, and he found the space cramped under the tables, particularly with the two thick plastic bags of loot hanging from his waist. Loose rubble kept falling in from the sides, roughing up the floor, piling a few inches high here and there to make the clearance even narrower. Marcantoni went through slowly, flashlight stuck out ahead of him, his eyes on that distant area beyond the last table, where it was still clear. He passed under the second table as Kolaski followed Angioni and then Williams followed Kolaski.

It was still falling, slight but relentless, the dry crap was still coming down, shifting this way and that. As Marcantoni reached the far end of the second table, a sudden cascade of dirt and dust streamed down in a curtain line from the narrow space between the tables, falling on his head and neck, blinding him. He jerked away, his shoulder hitting a table leg and jostling the table an inch to the left, as Mackey started to crawl after Williams, carrying the second flashlight.

More dirt fell. Marcantoni, unable to see anything, dropped the flashlight while trying to hold his hands over his face, keep the dirt out of his eyes. But the dirt was tumbling faster now down through the hole he'd widened, and more was sliding in from the sides. He kicked out, the plastic bag on his left side struck against something, and he hit the middle table. Now all three tables were awry, and the dirt thudded down into all that newly available space.

Parker was about to crawl after Mackey when Mackey abruptly backed out, one forearm over his eyes. A dust cloud followed him. Mackey veered right-ward out of its way, held the light aimed into the dark-ness under the table, and said, "Something's wrong. Something's gone wrong."

Parker crouched, looking where Mackey aimed the

light down the line beneath the tables, and they both saw nothing but the dust in there, and a spreading fall of dirt, and Williams' legs writhing, as he struggled for purchase, as he tried to pull back from the dirt that was burying him.

"Hold the light on me," Parker said, and slid in under the first table, crawling forward till he could reach Williams' thrashing ankles. He grabbed the ankles, pulled, pulled harder, and finally Williams' body began to slide along the brick floor.

Parker kept pulling, until Williams was back far enough that he could help with his own arms. Parker backed out of the narrow space, holding his breath against the dust cloud Williams caused by his movements, and Williams backed out after him, covered with dirt. "My God," he said, and coughed. "I was a dead man."

Mackey said, "The others?"

"It was Tom got in trouble first," Williams said, "and then everybody else. I don't think anybody got out, man."

Bricks fell near them. They backed away, Mackey shining the light at the rupture in the ceiling, which was larger now, more dirt falling down. "We're not gonna get to those guys," he said.

Williams said, "I don't know how you even got to me, but I'm grateful. I owe you my life."

Parker shook his head. "I didn't do it for you," he said. "Forget all that. I'll give you the truth here. What

I need is a crew, the more the better. I wish I could have those three back." Looking around at the useless tunnel, he said, "Because we're going to have to cut that armory back there a new asshole. We have to find a new way out of there."

THREE

1

Parker, disgusted, removed his belt so he could let the full plastic bags fall to the brick floor of the useless tunnel. Mackey watched him, frowning, then said, "You're leaving the swag?"

Sliding the belt back through the loops, Parker said, "What do we do with it? The people who knew who to call in New Orleans are down in there, under the dirt."

"God damn it," Williams said, "we don't have the customer."

"We don't have anything," Parker told him.

He hadn't liked this thing from the beginning. Mostly, it had been the simple matter that he hadn't wanted to stay in this part of the world after getting out of their prison, but he also didn't like to be pressured into doing something he felt wrong about.

And it had felt wrong to him, all the way. He hadn't known why, or what to look out for, but from the minute Marcantoni introduced the idea, back in

Stoneveldt, when it was clear to Parker that he had to agree to be part of this thing or lose Marcantoni—and he'd needed Marcantoni even more then than he needed him now—Parker believed it was all going to turn sour, one way or another, before he could get clear of this place. He'd never thought Marcantoni or the others would try to keep it all for themselves, when the time came to split up the proceeds; they were more professional—and sensible—than that. But he could feel it, out there, hovering. Something.

And here it was. A building that was famous for having only one way out, and now they had to find another way.

Williams was looking up at that long ragged split in the ceiling. "The street's up there," he said. "Suppose we could get up and out that way?"

Mackey said, "Dig a hole *upwards,* over my head? Into a street full of traffic? I'll stand over here and watch."

Parker said to Williams, "That doesn't work. Even if it doesn't cave in, and it probably wouldn't, you've got a hundred fifty years of paving up there, layer over layer of blacktop."

Mackey said, "That's why, when they want to get through it, they use a jackhammer."

Williams stopped looking up. With a shrug, he said, "That's the only idea I had."

Parker said, "We'll go back the way we came, see what we find."

The other two got rid of their plastic bags of jewelry,

and they left the tunnel, went back through the mostly abandoned storage room, and into the green-tinged parking area, where Mackey said, "Maybe it would be easier to get out down here. There's more garage space past this, for people who live in this place."

They walked over to the exit, which was covered by a heavy metal mesh gate that lowered from a drum overhead. Through the mesh, they could see the ramp extend upward toward the street, and a bit of the dark night up there.

But there was no way through or under or around the mesh. The barrier was seriously alarmed, firmly seated into deep metal tracks on both sides, and flanked by concrete block walls two layers thick. Above, the walls met a massive ceiling that was part of the original parade field inside the Armory, capable of bearing the weight of a company of horses, or tanks.

"We don't get out down here," Parker decided, and they went back upstairs, through the door Marcantoni had opened and Kolaski had unalarmed. Just inside that door, they stopped to look around. Halls extended away ahead of them, toward the display area where they'd been, and to both left and right.

Mackey said, "I think we gotta explore all these doors along here."

Williams said, "They won't lead out."

"Maybe we'll find something we can use," Mackey told him, and gestured to the hall on the right. "I'll take a look down there."

Williams said, "Parker?" Pointing at the two halls, he said, "You want this one, or that one?"

"I'll do the one straight ahead."

They separated, and Parker went forward to the first door on the right, which was closed. Opening it, he felt a wave of warm air come out, and when he found the light switch beside the door he saw that this was where the company's on-line operation was kept. The room was mostly empty, with free-standing metal shelves along both side walls like the ones fronting the tunnel door back in the library. On the shelves were bulky dark metal boxes that ran the wholesaler's Web site, displaying the wares and making the deals with customers anywhere in the world.

The machines also gave off heat, which was drawn away by a fan inside a metal grid high on the opposite wall. Mackey still had the flashlight, so Parker went down the hall until he found an open door with an ordinary office inside, took a gooseneck lamp from there, and carried it back to the Web site room. The outlet he found in there gave him just enough cord so he could aim the lamp through the grid to see what was inside.

A powerful-looking fan, attached to a solid iron A-frame, was mounted in the middle of a rectangular galvanized duct, about thirty inches wide and fifteen inches high. Using the lamp, he couldn't see very far into the duct, but it did go upward at a fairly steep angle, straight back from the grid.

It had to exit the building. It would angle up until it got above the ceiling of the other rooms back here, then run straight to an outer wall. Some sort of screen would have to be set up at that far end. With bars on the outside? Some sort of protection, anyway.

It would be a very tight fit, and it might have some impossible corners in it, and it could end at an opening it would be impossible to get through. There had to be something better than this.

Parker left the lamp on the floor in there and tried the door across the hall. The mail room, plus copier and fax. Nothing of interest.

The other four rooms along this hall also offered nothing of use. One near the front was where the staff took its breaks, with a refrigerator, coffeemaker, sofas, and chairs. The refrigerator contained some snack foods, which they might get to later on.

But not much later on; they couldn't afford to stay in this building a whole lot longer. They'd started this operation a little after six, and it was nearly eleven now. If they were still in this place after five in the morning they were in deep trouble.

The other three rooms were offices of various kinds; accountant, manager, and personnel, it looked like. Parker went through all the desks, but found nothing that looked like a control to open the garage exit downstairs, which would have been a simple way out. But nothing.

He was coming out of the last room, the manager's

office, when Mackey came down the hall, saying, "You know what you've got down there to the right, you've got an apartment."

Parker said, "Somebody lives here?"

"I don't think so," Mackey said. "Not usually. It looks like the owner, a guy named Jerome Freedman from what it said in there, things I looked at, he keeps the place for any time he might want to stay over in town, or maybe when they do inventory here, or whatever. But it's a complete one-bedroom apartment with a full kitchen. Looks as though nobody's used it for a while."

Parker said, "Anything useful in it?"

Mackey grinned. "You mean, like a buzzer to open the garage gate? I looked, believe me."

"And I looked around here," Parker said, as Williams came down the hall.

Mackey turned to him, saying, "I've got the owners' apartment, what've you got?"

"Storage rooms," Williams said, "and down at the end, a gym, with exercise machines. Nothing to give us a damn bit of help."

Parker told them about the duct in the Web site room, but neither of them wanted to explore that route. "It's the big room we want," Mackey said.

So they went back to the room with the display cases, many of them now with shattered glass, making jagged reflections in the small lights. Without discussion, they moved out into the dim room, each studying the place on his own, seeing it in a different way from the first time they'd come in here.

Parker moved to the right, to the exterior side wall of the building. This room was thirty-six feet long, with four windows spaced evenly along this wall. The windows were a foot wide and four feet high, with arched tops, and started at chest height. They were inset into the middle of a wall four feet thick, with decorative wrought-iron bars on the outside. Parker looked out at nighttime traffic, silent from in here, and the street seemed very far away. The deep-set narrow windows were like looking through the wrong end of binoculars.

So the windows were too narrow, too deep, and too barred to be of any use. Parker moved around to the front, with three more windows exactly like the others, and came to Williams looking at the closed front door. Through the glass they could see a brushed-steel articulated panel closed down over the entryway, the same as the one they'd seen earlier downstairs at the garage entrance.

Parker said, "We can't do anything in this direction."

"I know," Williams said. "But I'm beginning to think we can't do anything in *any* direction. If we could break through that, we don't care if it sets off alarms, or if the doorman out there hears us. If we get through, we take off."

"But we won't get through," Parker said. "Not here. It would take too long and it would make too much noise. The doorman could have the law here before we had the thing opened up."

From above, Mackey's voice called, "You can forget the ceiling."

Parker looked up, and Mackey had climbed ladder rungs mounted into the front wall. He was standing on the metal gridwork up there, holding a vertical support and looking down. He shook his head, and called to them, "Standing here, the ceiling's still too far away to touch. I don't know if there's anything up there might help us, but there's no place to get a whack at it."

Parker said, "Then it has to be something down here."

As Mackey came back down the ladder, Williams said, "What about a fire?"

"I don't think so," Parker said.

Jumping the last few feet, Mackey said, "You don't think what?"

Parker said, "Williams thought, maybe start a fire, we go out when the firemen come in."

Williams said, "If nothing else works."

"I don't know," Mackey said. Looking around, he said, "It'll take them a while to get in, won't it? We're down with smoke inhalation, they're still banging away with axes."

Parker said, "That's the problem, we'd have to make it a big enough fire to get noticed, but not big enough to knock us down."

Pointing at the left side wall, Mackey said, "If there's a way, it's there. The other side of that is the dance studio."

Williams said, "That's the new wall they put in when they converted. It won't be as tough as these outside walls."

"The only thing," Mackey said, "is mirrors. Brenda told me, they've got the big workout room where she was, it's got a whole mirrored wall. If we hit a mirror ten feet by twenty, it'll make a sound when it comes down, and *somebody's* gonna hear it."

Parker said, "What else did Brenda tell you about the dance studio?"

"Not much," Mackey said. "You know, she wasn't casing it, she was just going there. Lemme see, there's an office up front, and one time she said, when she's looking at the mirror in the room where she was taking the classes, she was thinking, all that jewelry's just the other side of that mirror."

Williams said, "Do we want to go up front, then, so we don't hit the mirror?"

Mackey shook his head. "I don't think so. It's gonna be too close to the lobby and the doorman, we don't want him to hear demolition."

Parker said, "Is it all studios along here?"

"I'm not sure." Mackey frowned, trying to remember. "I think the big room where she was, it was maybe third back. First the front office, then a locker room where they changed, and then the big room with the mirror.

And beyond that I think there's smaller rooms, but I don't know. And I don't know about any more mirrors."

Parker said, "What about all the way back? Williams, what's at that end of the hall?"

"The gym," Williams said. "The end door opens into it, and it's across that whole space."

"Same kind of wall as this?"

"Painted Sheetrock, yeah. There's mirrors, but they're on the back wall."

"If we go through at the rear corner back there," Parker said, "we might be able to figure out what the wall's made of before we go too far in."

Williams said, "There's tools in the janitor's closet along that hall."

"Good," Parker said. "Let's see what we've got."

The three left the main room and went back down the hall to the door they'd come in from the stairs, then turned right and Williams led them to the janitor's closet, with brooms and mops and an electric floor polisher on one side, shelves piled with cleaning supplies on the other. Part of one shelf was tools; two hammers, a pliers, half a dozen screwdrivers. They took everything and went to the end of the hall, where Williams opened the door and they went on into the gym, which was dark.

"We need light," Parker said. "No matter what happens." He found the switch beside the door, and fluorescents in the ceiling flicked on, showing a broad white room with black composition flooring. One of the tall narrow windows was in the wall to the left, with a long mirror fastened beside it. Exercise equipment stood on the floor or was fixed to the walls. To the right were a bathroom and a storage closet. Attached to the wall that interested them were weights with pulleys. Mackey went over to look at how they were held in place, and said to Parker, "This has got to be a pretty good wall, if it takes this. Just screws into studs, with all this weight and people pulling on it, some-body'd yank it right out."

"I'm guessing concrete block," Williams said.

Parker said, "There's one way to find out." Crossing to the far left corner, where the dance studio wall met the rear of the building, he swung the claw of the ham-mer into the white-painted Sheetrock, twisted, and pulled away a long vertical powdery V of the panel. He slashed at it again, this time crosswise, and a second zigzag piece broke free. Behind it was one-by-three lath, attached to gray concrete block.

Parker nodded at it. "That's what we have to go through," he said. "Before morning."

2

The only way to attack this wall was to go after the mortar between the blocks of concrete. To do that, they had to wedge a flat-head screwdriver against the mortar, as though it were a chisel, and hit it with the hammer. They worked two abreast, one hitting a vertical line, the other the horizontal line below it to its left, hitting the mortar leftward, to spray the wall beside them.

It went so slowly it didn't look at first as though anything was happening at all. Gray dust and rubble formed on the black floor, but how much had they removed? A quarter of an inch? Half an inch? Williams took over from Parker, and Mackey from Williams, and then Parker again, and they were no more than two inches into the mortar below and beside that one block.

Mackey was resting again, watching the other two at work, when he said, "A concrete block's eight inches thick. Those screwdriver blades are four inches long."

They stopped to look at him. Williams said, "We don't accomplish anything if we only go halfway."

"Let me see what I can find up front," Mackey said, and took the flashlight and left.

Parker said, "We might as well keep going."

To hit the mortar at an angle shortened the reach of the screwdrivers even more. They were three inches deep into the wall, and nearly at the end of the screwdrivers' reach, when Mackey came back with two lengths of chrome-covered metal. They were parts of the frame of one of the display cases that he'd broken off by bending them backward and forward, leaving jagged ends. They were L-shaped, less than an inch on a side.

"Let me straighten these," Mackey said. Taking one of the hammers, he laid first one, then the other, length of metal on iron weights taken from the exercise equipment and hammered the right angle out of them. Finished with that, he bent each length over on itself and hammered the crease. "Now," he said, "we can get in there with the V of the bend, scrape it back and forth. Slower than the screwdrivers, but it should break up the mortar."

It did. They used small towels from the gym closet to protect their hands, and scraped back and forth into the narrow slits they'd already made with the screwdrivers, pulling the crumbled mortar out, two working at a time, the third resting.

They'd been at it just over an hour when Parker, at the horizontal line, suddenly stopped and said, "It's through. Mackey, give me something to mark the metal."

Mackey gave him a screwdriver, and Parker scored the metal where it met the concrete block. "We know that's how far to go. We don't want to push too hard. We need to know what's beyond this."

It was only a few more minutes before both slits appeared to be through to the far side of the block, where they could feel an empty space back there. They started on the other two sides of the same block, the left and the top, and it went faster now that they knew how to do it. It was tiring work, and it felt hot in the gym, even with the thermostat off and the hall door open, but they kept working, and in just under an hour the block suddenly lurched downward, shutting the slit beneath it, widening the space above.

The problem now was how to get a purchase on the block to pull it out. Parker tried wedging the hammer claw into the top space to pry it out, but the block wouldn't lever, it just dug hard against the block below it. They had to come at it from the sides, pounding one hammer's claw into the space with the other hammer, prying it out, feeling the block move an eighth of an inch, then wedging the hammer in on the other side to do it again.

This part went even more slowly, or at least it seemed that way. It was very hard work, to force the hammer in, force the block to move, a small and grudging move every time. When it was out an inch, protruding from the wall around it, Williams crouched beneath the loose block to push up on it while Parker and Mackey pressed the heels of their hands against the exposed sides and tried to lever it out.

But it was too soon, they couldn't get enough purchase on it. They had to go back to the hammers, taking turns, beating the claw into the space, prying out, the block not seeming to move at all. Finally, when it was two inches out, twice as far as the first time, they tried again, doing it the same way, and this time the block suddenly jolted out another inch, and then another.

Williams got out of the way, and Parker and Mackey juked the block out by hand, back and forth, back and forth, hearing it scrape along on the mortar rubble, pulverizing it more. They got it almost all the way out and it hung there, angled downward, the top edge against the bottom edge of the block above.

Parker said, "We'll both pull out, bottom corners."

They wrenched, and the block jumped out of the space to fall hard onto the floor. Williams picked it up and carried it out of the way while Mackey shone the flashlight into the oblong hole. "Sheetrock," he said, seeing it an inch beyond the end of the concrete block wall, one furring strip a vertical line of wood near the right edge.

Mackey scraped the Sheetrock with the jagged edge of the metal bar. "I think there's something else behind it. Hold on, let me try. Parker, take the flashlight, will you?"

Parker held the light on the rectangle of Sheetrock and Mackey worked the bar back and forth, scraping away Sheetrock, trying not to simply puncture it. "Yeah, there's something." He prodded some more, breaking strips of Sheetrock away, and they looked through at another surface beyond the Sheetrock, dull white.

"Tile," Parker said. "It's a tile wall."

Mackey reached in to pull a strip of the Sheetrock away. He held it in both hands and they looked at the face of it, which was pale green. "It's waterproofed," Mackey said. "We found a bathroom."

Williams said, "We won't know if there's a mirror on it until we break it."

"A mirror in a bathroom," Mackey decided, "this far to the back of the building, isn't gonna wake anybody up. If it comes down to it, I'll volunteer for the bad luck."

"We've all got the bad luck already," Williams told him. "Parker and me, we already broke out once, and here we are again."

Picking up a hammer and screwdriver, Parker said, "We're running out of time," and went back to work.

3

The others were easier to get at, but still hard work. It was almost three in the morning before they'd removed the six blocks they needed to get out of their way; the one just above waist height they'd done first, then the two centered below that, the one below that, and the two below that. Now they had an opening in the wall thirty-two inches high and effectively sixteen inches wide.

"Shine the light," Parker said, and went to one knee in front of the opening. The bottom of it was just about at knee height; Parker reached in with the hammer and rapped a tile just above the next lower concrete block. He had to hit it twice, but then it cracked and fell backward, taking parts of two other tiles with it.

They looked through the new small hole into the darkness beyond, the flash gleaming on something glass, near to them, pebbled to bounce and refract the light. Mackey said, "What the hell is that?"

"A shower stall," Parker said. "That's the door."

"A nice door," Williams said. "At last."

Now that they knew there was nothing except the tile in their way, they quickly hammered it out of there, then clawed the one furring strip in their space with a hammer, weakening it so they could snap it in the middle and break the pieces off at top and bottom. Now they had a new doorway.

Mackey went through first, with the flash. The other two followed, as Mackey opened the shower door and stepped out to the bathroom. He switched on the lights there, and Williams said, "I think we oughta turn out the light behind us. No need to attract attention before we have to."

"Good," Parker said.

They waited while Williams went back to switch off the gym lights, then came back through the new opening to join them in what turned out to be an apartment connected to the dance studio.

"All these people," Mackey said, "they build themselves little nests at work, and then don't use them."

Williams said, "Better for us if they don't."

Once out of the bathroom, they limited themselves to the flashlight, moving through the rest of the dance studio area. They were out of the jeweler's now, but they were still inside the Armory, and the problem of getting out was still the same. The exterior walls on all sides were impregnable, windows too narrow to be useful, and a twenty-four-hour doorman at the only exit. And time running out.

Moving through the dance studio, they went first through the small neat apartment, then the offices, then the studios themselves. They saw the long mirror Brenda had told Mackey about, and Mackey laughed at it: "We coulda called attention with *that* thing."

The receptionist's room at the front was faintly illuminated by streetlights. A mesh barrier was closed over the front window and door; not impossible to get through but impossible to get through immediately and without noise.

As they turned away from that useless exit, Williams said, "We gotta get next door, into that lobby."

Mackey said, "Not another wall. Don't give me another wall."

"Maybe there's a door," Parker said.

There was. It took them twenty minutes to find it, but then there it was, a spring-locked door on the far wall of the main office, toward the rear, just in front of the apartment. The door opened inward; Parker pulled it ajar, just enough to look through, and saw the lobby, dim-lit, with elevators nearby to the left and the front entrance far away at the other end of the low-ceilinged space.

Parker stepped back, letting the door shut. "That's the lobby," he said. "But I can't see the doorman from here, and you know he's going to have video monitors."

"Lemme look," Williams said. "I'm pretty good at finding those things."

He hunched in the doorway, peering through the narrow space, then leaned back, shut the door, and said, "Two. One over the doorway this side of the desk, aimed at the elevators, and one over the elevators, aimed at the front."

Parker said, "And the stairwell door, that's just this side of the elevators."

"He'll see it," Williams said, "on his monitor."

Parker shook his head, angry at the obstacles. "If we try to just go straight through the front, deal with him along the way . . ."

"He'll be on the phone," Williams said, "before we can get to him. We could *get* to him, but the cops would be on the way."

Mackey said, "We don't want that kind of footrace."

"There has to be a way past him," Parker said. "If we can get into the stairwell, get down to the parking area, *that's* not gonna have security as tough as everything else around here."

Williams said, "He'll have a monitor shows him the garage."

"If we don't take a car," Parker said, "if we just walk out, walk along the side wall and out, we won't give him a reason to get excited. But first we've gotta get down there."

"Somebody switch on the lights in here," Mackey said, "I got an idea."

Parker had the flashlight. He shone it across the room, found the light switch by the opposite door, and crossed to turn it on. Two lamps on side tables made a warm glow, showing walls filled with prints of various kinds of dancers, in performance.

Mackey went to the desk, sat at it, lit a lamp there, and looked in drawers until he found a phone book. He leafed through it, read, and gave the open page a satisfied slap. "That's what we like," he said. "Twenty-four-hour service."

Parker and Williams sat in comfortable chairs in front of the desk while Mackey pulled the phone toward himself, dialed a number, waited, and then said, "Yeah, you still delivering? Great. The name's O'Toole, I'm in the Armory Apartments, apartment C-3. I want a pepperoni pizza. Oh, the eight-inch. And a liter of Diet Pepsi, you got that? Great. How long, do you figure? Twenty minutes, that's perfect."

He hung up and grinned at them. "By the time they work it out, we're in the stairwell, and this goddam place's history."

It was twenty-five minutes. They had the office lights switched off again, and took turns watching through the narrow crack of the open door, and at last they heard the building's front doorbell ring and heard the sound of the chair as the doorman got to his feet.

The delays were grinding them down. They had to get out of here before it was morning and the world was awake and in motion, but every time they moved they were forced to stop again. Stop and wait. All three of them had nerves jumping, held in check.

Five seconds since the doorbell rang. They stepped out of the office, single file, moving on the balls of their feet. They angled across the dim lobby and through the door into the stairwell.

Where the stairs only went up.

4

Parker said, "It's the goddam security in this place. They don't want anybody in or out except past that doorman."

"Well," Mackey said, "that's what people want nowadays, that sense of safety."

Williams said, "Bullshit. There's no such thing as safety."

"You're right," Mackey told him. "But they don't know that."

Parker said, "That *can't* be the only way in or out, because garbage has to go out, and they're not gonna send it out the front door. And deliveries have to come in."

Mackey said, "It seems that way."

"The fire code," Williams said. "They can't have a building this big, full of people living here, and only one staircase."

Parker said, "So there has to be service stairs, leading to a service entrance. We go up one flight here, we look in the halls, we find that other way."

Williams said, "What if there's video cameras in the halls, too?"

"Can't be," Mackey said. "It's too big a building, and one lone doorman. He can't look at fifty monitors."

"We'll check it out," Parker said, and started up the stairs.

This first flight was double in length, with three landings, to bring them higher than the ceiling of the former parade field next door. When they reached the first door, it had a brass 2 on it.

Stepping past Parker, Williams said, "Let me look for cameras."

They waited, while Williams cautiously pulled the door open and looked out, moving his head from side to side rather than stretch out into the hall. Then he opened it wider, leaned out, looking, and shook his head back at Parker and Mackey. "Nothing."

"Like I said," Mackey reminded them.

They went out to a crossing of hallways, all quietly illuminated. The elevator bank was to their right, a hall extended to their left, and another hall ran both forward and back. A plaque on the wall facing the elevators read RENTAL OFFICE, with a bent arrow to show the office would be at the end of the hall to the front.

Without speaking, they went the other way, because

the service stairs, if they existed, would be at the rear of the building. They moved silently, on pale-green carpeting, past apartment doors with identifying numbers and peepholes.

The door at the end of the hall had neither; instead, in small black letters, it said EMERGENCY EXIT. They went through into a barer, more utilitarian stairwell, all concrete and iron. At the bottom was a concrete landing with a broad metal door beside another of those tall narrow windows. The door had a bar across its middle to push it open, but the bar was bright red, with its message in block white letters: WARNING. WHEN DOOR OPENED, ALARM WILL SOUND.

Williams said, "Well? Do we push and run?"

Parker shook his head. "With no place to go to ground? Look out there, that street's empty."

Williams frowned out at the late-night emptiness, the closed stores across the street, this being a narrower street than the one in front. "Everywhere we go," he said, "there's something to stop us."

They were all silent a minute, looking out at the empty dark street, then Mackey, sounding reluctant, said, "What if I call Brenda?"

Parker said, "To come pick us up, you mean."

"I don't like her in these things," Mackey told them, "but maybe this time we gotta. She drives over, we see the car, go out, let the alarm do what it wants to do, Brenda drives us *away* from here."

Williams said, "I can't think of any other way."

"Neither can I," Mackey said.

Parker looked out. No traffic. "Then that's what we'll do," he said.

5

Parker hated going back, but there was no choice. Turn around, go up the stairs, the other way along that hall, toward the rental office. Instead of getting out of the maze, turn around and go back into the maze. And less time than ever.

The rental office door was locked, but not seriously. They went through it, and found a suite of offices illuminated by a few pale narrow strips of light. The tall thin windows continued up here, though not in the apartments farther up, and these windows were just above the level of the streetlights outside. It was their glow, coming through the deep-set narrow windows, that made the stripes of light across ceiling and desks and walls.

Mackey sat at the nearest desk, just outside a band of light, and opened drawers until he found the local phone book, then called the place where Brenda was staying. He spoke with the clerk there, then hung up, shook his head, and said, "She's got a no-disturb until her wake-up call at eight."

"We need a car," Parker said. "We need somebody with a car."

"Shit," Williams said.

They looked at him. Mackey said, "You got something?"

"I hate to think I do," Williams said. "I called my sister, you know, I went—"

"No," Parker said. "We didn't know."

"It wasn't dangerous," Williams promised him. "I left that beer company place where we were staying, late at night, I walked maybe five blocks, found a phone booth, called from there, came back. Nobody saw me, no sweat."

Parker said, "The law is listening to your sister's phone."

"I know that," Williams said. "I was just calling to say goodbye, because I gotta get away from here." He looked around at the rental office. Disgusted, he said, "If I ever get away from *here*, I mean, then I gotta get away from this town."

Mackey said, "You can't call your sister again. She would *definitely* bring the cops down on us. Not meaning to; they'd just come along."

"No, I wouldn't do that," Williams told him. "I wouldn't do a thing to mess up her life. But the thing is, when I called her, she told me, there's this guy we both know, his name is Goody, or everybody calls him

Goody, he already been in touch with her, soon as he heard I busted out, said to her she couldn't help me because of the cops but he could, give me money, whatever, I should call him, he'd help out."

Mackey said, "This is a good guy? Friend of yours?"

Williams shook his head. "This is a scumbag," he said. "He's a dealer, street dealer, works for some big-deal drug guy."

Parker said, "So he told your sister, have Brandon get in touch with me, I wanna help him, but what he means is, he'll turn you in."

"Sure," Williams said. "I knew that from the first second. I wasn't gonna call Goody at all. But now, maybe so."

Mackey said, "If you call this guy, tell him where we are, he just calls the cops, tells *them* where we are, goes back to bed, goes downtown tomorrow to collect the reward."

Williams said, "Well, I'm the only local guy in this room, and he's all I got."

Parker said, "Then we'll work with him."

Williams looked at him. "How?"

"You'll tell him a story."

"What story?" Williams spread his hands. "Soon as I tell him to come here, he knows I'm here."

"You don't tell him to come here," Parker said.

Mackey said, "Then what good is he?"

"Just wait," Parker told him. To Williams, he said, "When we were looking out that back way, across the street, there were stores. There was one of them, second or third in from the corner, a camera shop, isn't it?"

"Oh, yeah," Williams said. "Yeah, I been seeing that all my life, it's, uh, Nelson's Lens Shop, that's what it's called."

"Okay." Parker went over to one of the other desks, saying, "Come on over. Let's write this down."

Williams sat at the desk, found a pen and a sheet of letterhead stationery, and Parker said, "You call this Goody. You tell him you're hiding out in Nelson's Lens Shop, but you've gotta get out of there, you've gotta be out in— How fast could he get here, if you woke him up at home?"

"Half an hour."

"Okay, good. You tell him—it's almost three-thirty now—you tell him you've gotta be out of there by four. You just can't stay after that, one way or another you've gotta get out of there, even if it means just walking down the street. You've got two thousand dollars for him, cash money, if he'll come right *now,* pick you up, drive you to— What's a place he'll believe you want to go to, hide out?"

Williams thought. "There's a little town," he said, "Stanton, about ten miles down the river, it's all black, dying town, just some old people still living there. I got a couple relations living down there, he'd believe me if I said I was gonna go hide out with them awhile."

Parker said, "And he'll believe you think you can buy him off with two grand."

Williams laughed. "So he thinks I'm stupid, and I think he's stupid."

"No," Parker said. "He thinks you're stupid, but you think he's greedy. If he thinks there's money in it from you, in cash, he'll take you where you want to go *first*, and then call the law."

Mackey said, "So we go down to that door, and what? Soon as he shows up, we run out there?"

"No," Parker said. To Williams he said, "You tell him, you're hiding in the back of the store. When he gets there, he should come over and knock on the door." To Mackey, Parker said, "That way, he's out of the car before we move. And we get to see if it's Goody or somebody else that shows up."

6

When Williams hung up, his grin was both nervous and confident. "He'll do it," he said.

From just listening to this side of the conversation, Parker believed Williams was right. Williams had been hushed and urgent throughout the brief call. "I'll tell you in the *car*, man!" he'd exclaim, every time Goody started asking questions. "If you don't get here, I just gotta go, I don't know where, I just gotta get outa here!" And at last, "Good man, Goody, Maryenne says I could count on you, see you, my man." And he hung up and gave them his grin.

Mackey said, "I know it's more comfortable in this place, but I wanna be down by that door."

They all did. They left the rental office, strode to the far other end of the hall, past the sleeping residents of the Armory Apartments, and trotted down the service stairs to the door with the alarmed bar. Williams leaned against the window frame, looking out that deep narrow space at the camera store across the street, and Parker and Mackey sat on the stairs to wait.

The feeling at the bottom of this stairwell was like being in the base of a mineshaft. Even though they were at street level, the sidewalk just the other side of that door in front of them, it felt in here as though they were buried much deeper in the earth than when they'd been in the tunnel. The feeling reminded Parker of his more than two weeks in Stoneveldt. He wanted out of here.

It was three minutes to four when Williams suddenly straightened, looking out the window. Reading his body language, Parker and Mackey both got to their feet, watching Williams as he leaned closer to the window.

"It's him," Williams said. His voice was hushed, as though he was afraid the man out there could hear him. Then he shook his head. "Get out the *car*, Goody!"

Parker and Mackey moved in close to look out past Williams' shoulders. A black Mercury, several years old, was stopped now across the street, in front of the camera store. Gray exhaust sputtered from the tailpipe. The driver was indistinct, but clearly alone in the car.

Mackey said, "What's he waiting for?"

"He's got to get out of the car," Parker said.

And then he did. The driver's door opened, the interior light switched on, and Parker could see a skinny black man, any age from twenty to forty, jiggling in nervous fidgety motions inside there. He pushed his door open, hesitated, looked around, then abruptly jumped out of the car. Exhaust still puffed from the tailpipe. The driver closed the door, but then leaned his chest against the side of the car and stared off at something to his right, down the street.

Mackey said, "What's he looking at?"

Parker took his S&W Terrier .32 from its holster in the middle of his back. "We'll be finding out," he said.

The other two both brought out their pistols, as Goody finally moved across the street. Jerking like a marionette, he hurried around the front of the Mercury and ran to the inset doorway of the camera store. As he knocked on the glass over there, Parker rammed his body into the barred door. It popped open, outward to the street. A great metal *scream* rose up, and Parker and Mackey and Williams ran out to the street.

Parker was already looking to his right as he came out past the door, and what was parked down there, a dozen car lengths behind the Mercury, wasn't the law. It was a dark green Land Rover, with three burly black men boiling out of three of its doors. They were all shouting, but nobody could hear anything with the scream of that siren laid over them all.

Already there were lights coming on in windows up above, and the three men from the Land Rover waved guns as they ran forward. The two from the front seat would be muscle, the one from the backseat brain. All three started to fire their guns as they ran, which meant the bullets went anywhere.

Parker stopped in the street, one step beyond the curb, aimed down his right arm, dropped the brain. Mackey and Williams were also firing. Parker looked toward the Mercury, and Goody was running for it, across the sidewalk from the camera store, reaching for the passenger door. Two-handed stance, Williams shot him through both closed windows, and Goody bounced off the car, sprawled on his back on the sidewalk, shards of window glass glittering around him.

The three from the Land Rover were all down. That was the better car. Parker ran for it, knowing Mackey and Williams had to see him, because he couldn't shout to them under the siren. Windows were opening upstairs, people staring down at the street, where three men were fallen in twisted positions, one lay spread-eagled on his back on the sidewalk next to a black Mercury, and three men with guns in their hands raced for a hulking dark Land Rover.

Still running, Parker half-turned, pointed to Williams running behind him, pointed to the driver's seat of the Land Rover; Williams knew this town. The three piled in, Mackey following Parker through the same door to the back seat, and Williams tore them away from there.

As soon as the siren was behind them, Parker said, "Go to ground. Don't drive a lot."

"Where we put the cars," Williams told him. "It's just down here."

Parker looked back. No law yet. They'd been out of the building less than a minute.

Williams drove without lights, nothing else moving on the street, and when he got to the parking garage he stopped to get the ticket that opened the barrier, then circled upward three stories before he finally found a space to park. Cutting the engine, he turned to the two in back and said, "I think the big guy was the one Goody worked for."

"He should have stuck to drugs," Parker said.

7

What now?" Mackey asked. "Do we get the Honda and drive out of here?"

"We move to the Honda," Parker said. "We don't want to be in this thing."

"That's right," Williams said. "They'll be looking for these wheels everywhere around here."

They left the Land Rover, Williams locking it and taking the keys, and walked down the ramp to the Honda. Mackey had the keys for that; he unlocked it and took the wheel, Williams beside him, Parker in back. Putting the key in the ignition, Mackey said, "So now what? Drive out of here?"

"Too early," Parker told him. "We'd be the only car on the street."

"And with three guys in it," William said.

"But we should be above the Land Rover," Parker said.

"Right," Mackey said, and drove them up the ramp,

past the Land Rover and one level more to an area that was no more than half full. He tucked the Honda in between two other vehicles, both larger, then opened his window, shut off the engine, and said, "What do they do after they find it, that's the question."

Williams said, "Do they search the whole building?"

"No," Parker said. "They've got too much to do. This is a big place, a lot of cars, and pretty soon they'll be thinking about the jewelry place."

Mackey laughed. "Pretty soon they'll have a lot to think about," he said.

Williams said, "But they've at least got to look around in here."

"Sure," Parker agreed. "They ask the cashier if any car went out since four o'clock, he says no. They make a pass up to the top and back down. We duck down below window level while they go by. There's no car alarms going off, nothing looks wrong, that's it."

"But," Williams said, "they leave somebody at the exit."

"Both exits," Mackey said. "Car, and pedestrian."

"They probably will," Parker said. "They're looking for three guys. When traffic starts, around six o'clock, I'll get in the trunk, Williams lies on the floor here in back, it's just one guy in the car."

"Or maybe," Williams said, "I just walk down and out, meet you two around the corner."

Parker said, "You got any useful ID on you?"

Williams grinned and shook his head. "I see what you mean. I'll lie down there on the floor."

"Wait," Mackey said. "I hear something."

"That was fast," Williams said. "Suppose somebody saw me turn in here?"

"Let's hope not," Mackey said. "Because then they'd search every car."

Parker said, "Could you be hearing a civilian?"

"I don't think so." Mackey leaned leftward, listening at his open window, then shook his head. "I think it's two cars. They're just easing along, coming slow up the ramp, taking their time. They're searching."

They all listened. Parker could now hear it, too, the low grumble of two cars throttled back, spiraling very slowly up the ramp.

Williams said, "This job was fucked up from the beginning, wasn't it?"

"It felt wrong," Parker agreed, "but we were stuck in it."

"Stuck in the job or stuck in the jail." Williams grinned back at Parker. "Some choice."

"They stopped," Mackey said. "So they're at the Rover. I'm closing the window now." And he did.

Parker said, "If they do like we thought at first, loop up, turn around, loop back down, we're all right. If they go up and they *don't* come back down, that means they're searching everything."

Mackey said, "Do we have a Plan B?"

Parker shrugged. "Only leave the car, go down the

stairs, see how hard it is to get through whatever
they've got to guard the exit."

"And be on foot," Williams added.

"I like Plan A better," Mackey said.

Parker looked out his window to the right. Being in
the backseat, he had the better view of the ramp curl-
ing up from below. It was gray concrete, flanked by the
rears of cars. He kept watching it.

They had nothing left to say, and with the window
closed nothing to hear. They stayed in silence, Parker
watching the ramp, the other two watching Parker,
and then the black-and-white cruiser nosed around
the curve and Parker said, "Down."

They all ducked low, Williams folding himself into
the footwell, Mackey doing a kind of slow-motion
limbo, squeezing himself under the steering wheel. In
back, Parker lay on the floor, looking now upward and
out of the left window, where he could see the double
row of car roofs coiling away and up. After a minute,
he saw the black roof of the cruiser move among the
other roofs, gliding up and out of sight. He watched,
and then said, "Only one went up."

"Other one with the Rover," Mackey said. "Calling
in." He sounded compressed.

They waited, two minutes, three minutes, and here
came the cruiser again, angling back down the ramp,
moving at the same slow pace. "Coming back," Parker
said. "Just looking it over."

"Good," Williams said.

The cruiser left Parker's angle of vision. He waited, then turned around to look down the ramp. "It's gone," he said.

Everyone climbed back into the seats. "Been a while since I breathed," Mackey said. "I'm gonna open this window again."

"All I want," Williams said, "is to be in a place I'm not trying to get out of."

8

After a while they heard the tow truck arrive, a deeper sound with more snarl in it. A while later, it went away again. Now there was nothing to do but wait for the world to wake up and start moving around.

They all napped from time to time, not getting much out of it, but they were all awake when they heard the first car engine start, probably two levels below them. Mackey looked at his watch: "Ten to six."

"We'll wait awhile," Parker said.

"Oh, yeah."

By 6:15, they'd heard half a dozen cars start up and drive away, none of them from this far up the ramp. Then Mackey said, "I think we could try it now."

"Fine," Parker said, and got out of the Honda, pausing with the door open to say, "Leave me in the trunk until we get there."

Climbing out of the passenger seat in front, Williams said, "And I'll stay on the floor."

"Close me in," Parker said to him. Going to the back of the Honda, he drew the Terrier from its holster, to have ready in his hand in case anything went wrong, and opened the trunk.

As Parker climbed over the rear bumper, Williams grinned at him and said, "I know why you want you in there and me on the floor in back."

Parker looked at him. "You're darker."

"Right. You set?"

Parker lay curled on his side. The trunk was a little messy, but mostly empty, and not too uncomfortable. He had to keep his knees bent. With his head cushioned on his folded left arm, right arm resting across his waist, weight of the Terrier on the floor, he was in a position he could maintain for a while. "Set," he said.

"See you there," Williams said, and shut the trunk.

Now he had only his ears to tell him what was happening. In the blackness, he felt the car dip when Williams got aboard, then heard the engine fire up, then felt a jolt as Mackey backed out of the slot.

The experience was different, done this way. Braking and accelerating seemed more exaggerated, turns more abrupt. Parker was more aware of the Honda going down a fairly steep slope than he would have been if seated in the normal way in the car. He felt the change when they leveled out at the bottom, and gripped the Terrier tighter, waiting for something to go wrong.

If Mackey was challenged, they'd quickly find

Williams in back. They'd know they were looking for three men, so would they open the trunk right away? If they did, he'd do what he could. If they impounded the car before searching it, took it away to their pound, he'd try to find the best moment to get out of here.

The car stopped. Was Mackey paying the cashier now, or answering questions? The car started again. It jounced heavily down to street level, turned hard, drove straight, jolted to a stop. Red light. They were out of there.

It was a twenty-minute drive, with red lights and turnings. At the end, the Honda stopped, the door slammed, there was a pause, the door slammed, the Honda jerked forward again, and again it stopped. The door slammed, and then a second door slammed, and the trunk lid lifted. Parker saw Williams raising the lid, Mackey behind him closing the overhead door. They were back at the beer distributor's.

Parker got out, stiff in a lot of his body, and put the Terrier away, as Mackey came back from the closed door, looking at his watch. "Still too early to call Brenda," he said, "with that block on her calls, so we can't get out of here yet."

"We need sleep," Parker said. "We'll stay here now, leave this afternoon."

Mackey nodded. "That's probably a good idea."

Williams said, "I'm taking off. I'm too itchy, man, I wanna get out of here."

Mackey said, "You got a place to go?"

"Out of this state," Williams told him, "then south, then I don't know."

Parker said, "You don't have the money you thought you'd have."

"I'll promote some."

Mackey said, "You want to take the Honda?"

Williams raised an eyebrow at him. "Yeah?"

"If it belonged to anybody," Mackey said, "it belonged to those other guys. Brenda's got wheels and Parker's gonna ride with us."

"Then I'll do it," Williams said. "Thanks."

Mackey said, "You sure you don't want to get some sleep first?"

"The other side of the state line," Williams told him, "I'll sleep like a baby."

"Then go for it," Mackey said.

Mackey opened the overhead door again, and Williams backed the Honda out into early dawn. He waved at them through the windshield, and Mackey slid the door shut.

Upstairs, in the former offices, is where they'd set up temporary housing for themselves, with cots, each of the six of them with his own room. Parker and Mackey went up there now, and Parker took off only his shoes before he lay down, Terrier under pillow, and went immediately to sleep. He woke reaching for the Terrier, but it was Mackey who'd come into the room, saying, "They arrested Brenda."

FOUR

1

ive me a minute," Parker said.

The functioning men's room was upstairs. Parker washed face and hands, then looked at his watch. Not quite nine-thirty; he'd been asleep less than three hours.

When he went downstairs, Williams was back, and so was the Honda. Williams and Mackey sat at the conference table with containers of coffee and a bag of doughnuts; Parker sat with them. "I thought you were gone," he said to Williams.

"I thought so, too," Williams said.

"He heard it on the radio," Mackey explained. "So he turned around and came back."

Williams' smile was weak. "I was almost to the state line," he said.

Parker looked at him. "Why didn't you keep going?"

"If it wasn't for you people," Williams said, "I'd still be in Stoneveldt, and then someplace worse after that, the rest of my life. That's one. You said, 'Take the

Honda, we don't need it,' that's two. You two make no difference between me and each other, that's three."

"Three's all we need," Mackey told him. "Tell Parker what you heard on the radio."

"I had it tuned in to a news station," Williams said, "to help me know what to watch for. They described everything in the Armory—they had our route pretty good—and they said they were pretty sure it was you and me, escaped from prison, that was part of the gang, because Tom Marcantoni was one of the guys they found dead."

"All three dead," Mackey said. "Like we thought."

"Then they came on," Williams said, "they said they had an arrest, I thought it was gonna be you two, but then they said it was a woman. Then I thought, it's Maryenne, it's my sister they're after because I called her that one time, but it isn't. They describe a white woman, and say the only name they have is an alias, Brenda Fawcett."

Parker shook his head. "What are they doing with Brenda? She was asleep in her hotel with a do not disturb."

"That's the bitch of it," Mackey said. "She wasn't. She pulled that trick again, that thing she does, where she hangs around near me in case I need help."

Parker said, "She was *out* there?"

"Most of the night," Mackey said. "Maybe a block away. If we could have reached her, she could have come right over in a minute."

"You told her," Parker said, "she was gonna make trouble for herself doing that one of these days."

"And when she went back to the hotel," Mackey said, "after we busted out and set off that siren, somebody saw her go in. But that isn't what did it."

Williams said, "Somebody else turned her in. The woman that runs the dance studio."

"I'm sorry now," Mackey said, "we didn't bust her goddam mirror."

Parker said, "The woman in the dance studio? What's *she* got to do with anything? And what've they got on Brenda that they're gonna pull her in?"

Williams said, "What they said on the radio, Brenda went to this dance studio a few times, took lessons, paid cash, gave a phony name, used phony ID."

"Now they're saying," Mackey said, "she was casing the joint. For us."

Williams said, "So this woman runs the dance studio, Darlene Something, one of those two-name things, she *followed* Brenda one time, see where she really lives, so when the cops call her this morning, tell her the dance studio's all messed up, or where we come through, she says, 'It's Brenda Fawcett, she's part of it.' And they go pick her up."

"And find," Mackey said, "a lot of fake ID I gave her a while back, just like to goof with."

"So now she's the brains of the gang," Williams said, "and they want her to tell them where the rest of us are."

"Parker," Mackey said, "I gotta get her out of there."

"I know that," Parker said.

"The radio says," Williams told them, "they're holding her at the Fifth Street station, until they find out who she really is and what she knows about the rest of us."

Mackey asked him, "Do you know this Fifth Street station?"

Williams grinned. "I put up there a couple times," he said. "It isn't the city jail, it's more of a holding tank kind of place. Connected to a precinct. You're there, and then they move you on to some place real, once they decide where you should go."

Mackey said, "Any place else would be tougher."

"Fifth Street isn't *easy*," Williams assured him.

"But you know the place," Mackey said. "You can give us the layout." Turning to Parker, he said, "We gotta get her out of there *today*. She isn't gonna like that place."

Parker didn't say anything. Mackey was about to turn back to Williams, but then he frowned at Parker. "Are you saying you aren't in this?"

Parker didn't want to be in it, he wanted to get away from this place, get back east, spend some time with Claire, decide what to do next. He'd been nailed to the floor here too long. He didn't have that feeling of obligation that had sent Mackey to give him a hand when he needed to get out of Stoneveldt, or that had made Williams turn around at the state line and come back into the pit he'd spent all this time crawling out of.

Parker didn't live by debts accumulated and paid off; but there were times when you had to do things you didn't want, be places you didn't want. He could stand up now and walk out of here and head east, and there'd be no problem, not now. Neither of these people would shoot him in the back as he got to the door. But somewhere down the line, Mackey would think about him again, and he'd have a different kind of IOU in his mind. Parker didn't collect the IOUs, neither the good ones nor the bad ones, but he knew he had to live among people with those tote boards in their minds.

"I didn't say anything at all yet," he answered Mackey. "I was thinking, we got to get hold of that lawyer Claire found me."

Mackey beamed. "You're right! Jonathan Li. He's the guy."

"I've still got his card, up with my stuff," Parker said, and got to his feet. "But we need to get us inside there, too. I don't know how yet."

He went upstairs to his room. In the few days they'd been out, they'd accumulated a small amount of possessions; some clothing, toilet articles. Parker's things were in the drawers of an abandoned wooden desk. He found the card and looked at it again, the many partner names in fine blue letters against ivory, the name Jonathan Li in gold at the bottom right. He carried the card downstairs, put it on the table, and said, "The problem is, none of us can go to him."

"I can phone him," Mackey said. "I'm not an escaped felon, where he might have to tell the law about me, I'm just somebody the cops want to talk to about people who *are* escaped felons."

"There's a payphone—" Williams started to say.

"No, I don't need that," Mackey told him. "Tom had a cellphone, it should be upstairs with his stuff. I'll be right back."

He left, and Williams looked at Parker, considering him. "You don't like this," he said.

"None of us likes it."

"Yeah, I know." Williams nodded. "But Mackey feels like he owes Brenda, and I feel like I owe you and Mackey, but you don't feel like you owe anybody anything. Tell you the truth, I wish I could be like that."

"If you were like that," Parker told him, "you wouldn't have phoned your sister."

"Meaning," Williams said, "one of these days I'm gonna do something like that, because I feel like I owe somebody something, and I'm gonna put my head right in the noose."

"Maybe not," Parker said, and Mackey came back downstairs with the cellphone.

"I don't know," he said, hefting the phone. "Is he in the office yet? I can't leave a callback number."

"Try," Williams said.

So Mackey sat at the table and punched out the

number, then listened, the cellphone a small black beetle against the side of his blunt head.

"Jonathan Li, please. Would you tell him it's a guy, he's so happy about how Mr. Li dealt with the Ronald Kasper problem, now he wants to hire Mr. Li on the Brenda Fawcett problem. Sure."

Mackey put his other hand over the mouthpiece and said, "He isn't in the office, but they can patch in to him. In his car, I guess, or wherever."

Then he bent to the phone again. "Mr. Li? Yes, this is Ed, you remember me." Shrugging, he said to the others in the room, "He's laughing." Then, into the phone: "Yeah, you're probably right. Yeah, that's what they said on the radio, Fifth Street station."

Raising his eyebrows at Parker, he said into the phone, "Sure, I think you can get a retainer from Claire again, same as last time. Probably easiest."

Parker nodded. Mackey said into the phone, "She wired it to your account last time, didn't she? So she'll do it again. You just tell me how much. Fine, tell me then. That's terrific. Nice to do business with you again, Mr. Li."

Mackey broke the connection, put the phone on the table, and said, "After he laughed, he told me he wasn't surprised there'd be a link between a friend of Ronald Kasper and a friend of Brenda Fawcett. He says he knows it's urgent, he'll go over to the Fifth Street station right now, let Brenda know he's her legal, he understands I'm probably somewhere he can't phone me so I should phone him in three hours. By then he'll know the situation, he'll tell us how much is the retainer."

"In three hours," Williams said. "Good."

Parker said, "We still have to get *us* into this Fifth Street station." Standing, he said, "I'm gonna spend the three hours asleep."

2

He wants to meet," Mackey said. He held the phone to his chest while he talked to Parker. The three of them were again at the downstairs conference table.

Parker said, "You're the one he wants to meet."

Mackey shook his head. "You should be along. We need to know the situation, what we should do."

"He doesn't want *me* anywhere," Williams said. "I'll wait here. You leave the phone with me."

Into the phone, Mackey said, "Two of us, but we gotta be careful. You don't want us in your office." He listened, then grinned at Parker: "He likes to laugh, this lawyer." Into the phone again, he said, "Good, that sounds good. Wait, give me the names."

There were a notepad and pen on the table, left over from some scheming by Angioni and Kolaski. Williams slid them over and looked alert, and Mackey said, "Fred Burroughs and Martin Hutchinson. Four o'clock. We'll be there." Hanging up, he said, "It's his club, downtown. He wants us to meet at the handball courts. He says it's loud there, lots of echoes."

"Nobody can tape," Parker said.

Mackey nodded. "That's the idea."

It wasn't easy for Parker and Mackey to turn themselves into people who might be accepted as a member's guests in a club downtown that featured handball courts, not after the twenty-four hours they'd just lived through, but they managed. Washed and shaved, in the clothes they'd planned to wear when they'd quit this town after the job, casual but neat, they left the beer distributor's at three-thirty and walked half a dozen blocks before they saw a cruising cab and hailed it. It felt strange to Parker to walk along the street in a town where every cop had just last week memorized his face, but the afternoon was November dark and Parker let Mackey walk on the curbside. They saw no law at all, and then they were in the cab.

The Patroon Club had a doorman, under a canvas marquee mounted from building to curb. He held open the cab door while Mackey paid the fare, then called them *sir* and walked with them under the marquee to the double entrance doors, where he grasped a long brass handle, pulled the door open, bowed with just his head, and said, "Welcome to the Patroon."

"Thanks," Mackey said.

Inside was a dark wood vestibule, coat closet with attendant on the left, low broad dark gleaming desk straight ahead, behind which sat an elderly black man in green and white livery. He looked alert, inquisitive, ready to serve: "Help you, gentlemen?"

"We're here to meet Jonathan Li," Mackey told him. "Fred Burroughs. And this is Martin Hutchinson."

"Oh, yes, Mr. Li left your names." Opening a folder on his desk, he said, "If you could just sign the register."

The register was a sheet of paper with columns to be filled in: name, date, time, company, member to be visited. They both wrote things, and the man behind the desk gestured at the inner door behind himself, saying, "Mr. Li said you'll find him by the handball courts. That would be straight through, down the stairs, and second on your right."

Mackey thanked him again, and he and Parker went through the door into a plush dark interior, just slightly seedy. Downstairs, they found three handball courts in a row like three stage sets, side walls not meeting the ceiling, windowed at the interior end to face bleachers where spectators could sit. Only the nearest court was in use, two players in their forties, both of them very fast and very good. They made noise, but not too much.

Li sat on the third row of bleachers, watching the game, then nodded when he saw Mackey and Parker come in. He patted the cushioned bench beside him, and they came over, Parker to take a seat at Li's right, Mackey choosing a place on the second row, just to their left, where he could sit sideways and look up at them both.

Li nodded to Parker and said, "Before we begin, just let me make the situation clear. I assume you did not come here trailing police—"

"No," Parker said.

"No, of course not. But to consider the possibility, however remote, if in fact we *are* interrupted by an official presence, I will explain that we were meeting to work on the details of your turning yourself in, and *you* will say the same."

"Naturally," Parker said.

"Good." Li turned to Mackey. "Now, to *your* friend. The police seem unable to learn her true identity."

"They never will," Mackey said.

"I begin to believe you're right. She was paying for her hotel room with a credit card under the Brenda Fawcett name. They have now learned from the credit card company that the bills are sent to an accountant in Long Island, who pays with money taken from the account of a client of theirs named Robert Morrison. They have not physically seen Morrison in some years, but send him statements to a maildrop in New York City. They manage a few money market accounts for Morrison, and he occasionally sends them more money— How, if I may ask? The police don't know, or at least didn't tell me."

"Money orders," Mackey said. "Every once in a while, top up the tanks with some money orders."

"So Ms. Fawcett is not their customer, nor can they directly reach Morrison, who pays her bills."

Mackey said, "Does she give them a story?"

"The police here?" Li smiled, almost in a proprietary way, as though it were a story he'd made up himself. "She says," he told them, "she is fleeing an abusive husband. Court orders didn't help, police protection didn't help—a little dig there, of which they are not unaware—she is in fear of her life, she will never give anybody at all her correct name for fear this man will find her." Li shrugged. "The police don't exactly believe her," he said, "but it isn't a story they can do anything about."

"Brenda's good," Mackey said. "She can do all the emotions: outrage, fear, just a little sex."

Parker said, "The point is, to get her out."

"Clean, if we can," Mackey added.

"When it comes down to that," Li told them, "as I've been pointing out to the ADA assigned to this case, a young woman with little experience and, if I may say so, no feel for the job, there is no crime here. When picked up this morning, at the hotel, Ms. Fawcett had clearly not spent the night crawling through walls and tunnels. Nothing to connect her to the Armory or to Freedman Jewels was found on her person nor in her hotel room—"

"Suite," Mackey said.

"I beg your pardon," Li said, and laughed. Mackey was right; he liked to laugh. "Her suite," he corrected himself. "Nothing in that fine suite to suggest its sole occupant was a common burglar. They have on their hands a suspicious situation, in that Ms. Fawcett will not reveal her true identity, nor have they been able to find her true identity on their own. Other than that, they have the testimony of Darlene Johnson-Ross—"

"The dance studio woman," Mackey interjected.

"Yes." Li nodded. "The source of all Ms. Fawcett's problems, if it comes to that. She is the one who informed the police that Ms. Fawcett has been operating in this city under a false name and background, and she is the one who claims to have seen Ms. Fawcett in a parked car a block from the Armory late last night."

Mackey said, "Took a picture?"

Li shook his head. "Drove by, alone, in a moving automobile, in the middle of the night. Saw, for an instant, not near any streetlight, a blonde at the wheel of an unmoving car. While, of course, she has been obsessing about a blonde she has seen at her dance studio. On the stand, I'd demolish that identification in three minutes."

Mackey said, "We don't want to go on the stand."

"Oh, I know," Li assured him. "We *should* be getting bail, we really should, since there's so little to tie Ms. Fawcett to the crime, except for the problem of identity. Still, I could make a strong case in front of a judge, and the police know it, and don't want to lose control of Ms. Fawcett until they find out who she is."

"Which is never," Mackey said.

"In the interim," Li said, "they've put up Ms. Johnson-Ross to file a complaint against Ms. Fawcett for false statements on a credit application."

Mackey said, "What credit application? Brenda paid cash."

"Exactly." Li spread his hands. "It's merely a plot to stall things, delay the release. A false statement on a credit application *is* a misdemeanor, but the form Ms. Fawcett filled out at the dance studio was *not* a credit application, since she was paying cash. It's simply a maneuver to keep her in their grasp."

Mackey said, "And this Johnson-Ross goes along with it?"

"She will, in the morning," Li told him. "They weren't quite ready today, and I was raising a number of objections, including the possibility that Ms. Johnson-Ross might find herself facing a severe lawsuit from Ms. Fawcett once this is all over, which led Ms. Johnson-Ross to say she'd need to consult her own lawyer before agreeing to make out the complaint, so that step has now been scheduled for ten tomorrow morning."

Mackey and Parker looked at each other. Catching the look, Li said, calmly, "Let me point out, the very worst thing that could happen to Ms. Fawcett's chances to successfully put this episode behind her would be for some unfortunate accident to occur before ten tomorrow morning to Ms. Johnson-Ross. The police don't believe in coincidence."

Mackey said, "So what do you do next?"

"Argue, dispute, disrupt," Li told him. "I will do my best to quash Ms. Johnson-Ross's complaint, I will do my best to have bail set, but, from the way it looks at this point, I'm afraid Ms. Fawcett will be facing at least one more night of detention."

"You'll do what you can," Mackey said.

Li shrugged. "Of course." From inside his jacket he drew a long white envelope printed with his firm's return address. "My retainer," he murmured.

Parker took the envelope and put it away. He said, "She'll send you an extra two K. You can give it to Brenda or one of us."

Li nodded. "I understand. Walking-around money."

"Moving-around money," Parker said.

3

At the beer distributor's, Williams had drawn maps of the Fifth Street station, exterior and interior, all four floors, the streets of that neighborhood. "I don't say it's complete," he warned them. "It's what I remember."

They stood at the conference table, looking at the half dozen rough pencil drawings on the backs of old order forms. Parker and Mackey hadn't had much to say to each other in the cab back to this neighborhood, nor the three-block walk through deepening dusk from where they'd left the cab, but now Parker said, "It's breaking out again."

"I know," Williams said. "All we do is break outa things. And now break this woman Brenda out."

Mackey said, "I don't want to do it that way."

Williams looked at him. "What other way is there? They got her in there. She's locked down."

"I don't know what the other way is," Mackey said.

"She's never been fingerprinted before. She's got no record, no *history* with the law. If we go in there and break her out, now she's got a history and now they've got her prints and now she can't live her life the same way she always did. There's got to be another way."

Parker said, "Li's right, the big problem is the dance studio woman."

"Yeah, she is," Mackey said. "But Li's also right that we can't touch her. It would make things worse for Brenda because, first of all, it would prove we're connected to her. If Ms. Johnson-Ross gets a cold sore tonight, Brenda's behind bars the rest of her life."

Parker said, "Well, we've only got two choices, unless we just walk away, and I know you don't want to do that."

"No, I don't," Mackey said, almost as though he wanted an argument.

Parker nodded at Williams' drawings. "We can either go into this Fifth Street station tonight and bring Brenda out, and she lives the way you say, the way you and I live, the way Williams lives, or we go see this dance studio woman, see what kind of handle we can put on her back."

Williams said, "What if you can't put any handle at all?"

"Then we remove her," Parker said, "and go pull Brenda out anyway. She won't be clean, but she'll be out."

"If that's what we gotta do," Mackey said, "then that's what we gotta do."

Parker shrugged. "Nothing's gonna happen right away. If we take it easy now, find out where this woman lives—"

"She'll be in the phone book," Mackey said. "Everybody's in the phone book."

Williams grinned and said, "Probably Brenda is, somewhere, under some name."

"That's what I'm trying to keep," Mackey told him.

Parker said, "We get up at three, three-thirty, go to this woman's place, see what we can do. Get her maybe to phone the cops in the morning, say she changed her mind, doesn't want to make any complaints, isn't even sure that was Brenda in the car."

Williams said, "They'll send somebody over to argue with her."

Mackey said, "I just thought. What if she lives above the shop? What if her place is one of the apartments in the Armory building?"

Williams laughed. "Well, we do know *that* place," he said.

Mackey said, "Parker? We go in *there* again?"

"That isn't where she lives," Parker said. "She had a little apartment in the studio, remember? For when she wants to stay over. Not her full-time place, not used much. So her full-time place is not in the same building."

"I hope not," Williams said.

"We'll see how it plays," Parker said, "and if it isn't *gonna* play, we'll go over to Fifth Street, still early in the morning, and pull Brenda out of there." He looked at Mackey. "Okay?"

Mackey nodded. "First we try it easy," he said.

Parker said, "Then we don't."

4

There was only one Johnson-Ross in the phone book:
JOHNSON-ROSS D B 127 Further R'town

"She's doing good for herself," Williams commented.

It was twenty to four in the morning, and they were seated again at the conference table. The phone book left behind by the beer distributor was three years out of date, but this was surely Johnson-Ross's current address. Parker said, "You know this place?"

"Rosetown," Williams told him. "North of the city. Pretty rich up there. Until a few years ago, if I was to drive through Rosetown, I'd get stopped sure. DWB."

Sounding interested, Mackey said, "Not any more?"

Williams shrugged. "Now it would depend on the car," he said.

Parker said, "So it isn't city police, it's a local force."

"Yeah, but they're rich," Williams said. "Those are people spend money on law enforcement."

"Which means the Honda's no good to us," Parker

said. "We need a car that'll make their cops comfortable."

"Well, I guess that's me," Mackey said.

They looked at him, and he said, "Brenda and me, we almost always go by car, but as much as we can, we leave the car out of it. Like we came here, we took it to the airport, left it in long-term, took a rental back."

Williams said, "What do you do that for?"

"If something happens to one of us," Mackey told him, "it doesn't happen to the car, so we're that far ahead. Like now; they got Brenda, but they didn't get a car. And a car would have another whole set of ID for the cops to play with."

Parker said, "What is this car?"

"Two-year-old Saab, the little one, red."

Williams laughed. "You'll look like a college boy coming home on vacation."

"Sounds right for that neighborhood," Mackey said, "doesn't it?"

Parker said, "So what we have to do, take the Honda to the airport, get this Saab."

"And once again," Williams said, "I'm on the floor in back."

There were two kinds of long-term parking; inside a brick-and-concrete building or, the cheaper way, in an outside lot. Mackey drove to the outside lot, picked up a check, and found the Saab in its place, small and sleek, gleaming in the high floodlights. Leaving the

Honda, he crouched beside the Saab, and from underneath drew a small metal box with a magnet on one side. Opening it, he took out the Saab's key and used it to unlock the car.

Once the metal box was in the glove compartment, the parking check was out of the glove compartment, the Honda was in the Saab's old space, and Williams was again on the floor in the narrow rear-passenger area, Mackey steered toward the electric exit sign, saying, "One thing. If we have to go on from the dance woman to the Fifth Street station, we don't use this. We go back to the Honda."

"It's your car and it's your woman," Parker pointed out.

From the floor in back, Williams said, "When you're out of the airport, take the left on Tunney Road, I'll direct you from there."

One-twenty-seven Further Lane was a bungalow, a one-story mansarded stucco house with porch, on a winding block of mostly larger and newer houses. Darlene Johnson-Ross had spent for the best neighborhood she could afford, not the best house.

The Saab drove by, slowly, seeing no lights, not in that house or any other house nearby. The dashboard clock read 5:27, and this wasn't a suburb that rose early to deliver the milk. They'd seen one patrolling police car, half a mile or so back, but no other moving vehicles, no pedestrians.

Most of the houses here had attached garages. The bungalow had a garage beside it, in the same style as the house, but not attached. Blacktop led up to it, then a concrete walk crossed in front of the modest plantings to the porch stoop. A black Infiniti stood on the blacktop, nose against the garage door.

As they went by, Parker said, "Go around the block, cut the lights when you're coming back down here, turn in, stop next to the other car."

"And then straight in?"

"Straight in."

They made the circuit without seeing any people, traffic, or house lights. Mackey slid the Saab up next to the Infiniti, half on blacktop and half on lawn, then the three moved fast out of the car and over to the front door, which Parker kicked in with one flat stomp from the bottom of his foot, the heel hitting next to the knob, the wood of the inside jamb splintering as the lock mechanism tore through.

They didn't have to search for Johnson-Ross; their entrance had been heard. As they came in, Williams paused to push the door as closed as it would go, and a light switched on toward the rear of the house, showing that they'd entered a living room, with a hall leading back from it. Light spilled from the right side of the hall, most of the way back.

They moved toward the hall, and ahead of them a male voice sounded, high and terrified: "Muriel! Oh, my God, it's Muriel!"

Then a female voice, more angry than frightened: "Henry? What are you *talking* about?"

Just entering the hall, Parker stopped and gestured to the other two. Everybody wait. It would be useful to listen to this.

The man's voice went on, with a broken sound. He was crying. "It's the detectives, I knew we'd never get away with it, you couldn't be alone tonight, not after— How could I have been so *stupid,* she called Jerome, she *knows* I'm here, all those lies—"

"Henry, *stop*! Muriel doesn't know anything because Muriel doesn't *want* to know anything! *What was that crash?*"

"Private detectives, I knew she'd—"

"Henry, get up and see what that was!"

Now the three moved again, down the hall and into the bedroom, where the couple, both naked, sat up in the bed, he babbling and sobbing, she enraged. They both stopped short when Parker and Mackey and Williams walked in and stood like their worst dream at the foot of the bed.

Parker said, "Henry, do we look like private detectives?"

The woman slumped back against the headboard, color drained from her face. "Oh, my God," she whispered.

Henry, not knowing what was going on if this was some nightmare other than the nightmare he'd been expecting, picked fretfully at the blanket over his knees as though trying to gather lint. "What do you—" he started, and ran out of air, and tried again: "What do you want?"

Parker looked at the woman. "You recognize us, don't you?"

"On the news," she whispered, still staring, still too pale, but recovering. "You"—and her eyes slid toward Williams—"and you."

Now Henry caught up: "Oh, you're *them,*" he cried, and for a second didn't seem as scared as before. But then he realized he still had reasons to be scared, and shrank back next to the woman. "What are you going to do?"

This was Mackey's game; Parker said to him, "Tell Henry what we're going to do."

"We're going to have a conversation," Mackey told them. "We're going to talk about poor little innocent Brenda Fawcett, pining away in a jail cell while you two roll around in your—adulterous, isn't it?—adulterous bed."

5

I knew she was part of the gang!" the woman cried, forgetting her own fear as she pointed at Mackey in triumph.

"But she wasn't," Mackey said. He was being very gentle, very calm, in a way that told the two on the bed he was holding some beast down inside himself that they wouldn't want him to let go.

The woman blinked. "Of course she was," she said. "She was casing the place."

"Casing the dance studio?" Mackey grinned at her, in a way that seemed all teeth. "Come on, Darlene," he said. "You know why she was there."

"She's with you people."

"She's with *me*," Mackey said. "Not doing anything, not *working*, you see what I mean? Just along for the ride." He gestured at Henry seated there now with mouth sagging open, like somebody really caught up in an exciting movie. "Probably like Muriel," Mackey explained, and Henry's mouth snapped shut, and Mackey said to him, "Right, Henry? Muriel's just along for the ride, not *part* of what you're doing, am I right?"

Henry shook his head. "I don't know what you mean."

"Then you're just not thinking, Henry," Mackey told him. In creating this dialogue, rolling it out, taking his time, Parker knew, Mackey was both easing their fears and keeping the pressure on. They were all in a civilized conversation now, so their survival seemed to them more likely, so they would gradually find it easier to go along with the program, and eventually to do what Mackey wanted them to do.

Rolling it out, Mackey said, "You're part of the bunch fixed up the Armory, right?"

Henry looked frightened again, as though this were a trick question. "Yes, I suppose so," he said.

"You got your father in there with his jewelry business."

Henry's lips curved down. "Yes, you'd know about that," he said.

Parker said, "We know about everything, Henry."

"You put Darlene here in the dance studio," Mackey went on, "and every once in a while you come around and dance. So there you are, captain of industry, putting together deals, making it happen. Muriel around for much of that, Henry?"

"What do you mean, *around?*" Henry's incomprehension was making him desperate. "I'm *married* to her."

"Sure, but was she at the meetings? When you and the guys were putting together the Armory deal, when you made the deal with your father, when you made the deal with Darlene here. Muriel in on any of that, Henry?"

"No, of course not," he said.

Mackey spread his hands: case proved. To Darlene, he said, "You get my point? I'm here, I'm working, my friend's along. She isn't working, she's just along, like Muriel. She gets bored, she takes a few classes over at your place. She can't give you real information about herself, because maybe something might go wrong with what I'm doing here, but she's paying you in cash, so it doesn't matter what she says. But then you decide, 'Hey, this woman is lying to me, I can't have that, I can't have some woman come into my dance studio and lie to me, I'm gonna find out what she's up to, and if I can make some trouble for her, I'll make some trouble for her.' Just like Muriel might get a little pissed off at you, Darlene, and if she could make some trouble for you, and I bet she could, what do you think? You think you can run a dance studio and have an alienation of affection suit going on at the same time, all in public, all over the cheap crap the press has turned itself into? And no help from Henry, you know, Muriel would be keeping *him* occupied, too."

"Oh, God," Henry said, and covered his eyes with one hand, head bowed.

There was a chair against the side wall, with some of Henry's clothing on it. Saying, "This is gonna take a while, these people are slow," Williams walked over to the chair, dumped the clothing off it, and sat on it.

Henry lowered his hand to gape at his clothes on the floor. Darlene said, "Even if—"

Mackey looked at her with polite interest. "Yeah?"

"Even if you're telling the truth," Darlene said, "even if she wasn't a *part* of it, she was *here* with you, she's still an accomplice."

Mackey said, "Is Muriel an accomplice? They still have those old blue laws on the books in this state, did you know that? Who knows how many different felonies you two already committed in that bed there, but the point is, is Muriel your accomplice?"

"That's absurd," she said.

"You're right," Mackey agreed. "And Brenda's my accomplice the same way."

She frowned, trying to find some way around this comparison, then impatiently shrugged and said, "It isn't up to me, it's up to the police. If whatever-her-name-is was *more* than just 'being around,' they'll find out."

"Oh, but that's the problem, Darlene," Mackey said. "It isn't the police that make trouble for Brenda, it's you."

"It's up to them now," she insisted. "If she wasn't doing anything wrong, they'll let her go."

"But they don't want to let her go, do they, Darlene?" Mackey asked her. "They told you themselves, they don't have a single thing to hold her on, but they don't want to let her go because they're suspicious of her because they can't find out who she is, so that's why they want you to go back tomorrow morning and sign a complaint against her."

Henry jerked to a crouch, hands clasped together, staring at Mackey as though he were some kind of evil wizard. "How did you know that?"

Parker said, "I told you, Henry. We know everything."

Darlene said, "They asked me to cooperate."

Mackey said, "To sign a complaint that she made false statements on a credit application."

"Well, they were false," she said.

Mackey shook his head. "It wasn't a credit application."

She started to snap something, angry and impatient, but then stopped herself, as though she hadn't realized till that second what the law had asked her to do. Maybe she hadn't. She shook her head, rallied: "They were false statements."

"Not on a credit application. Not a crime."

Until now, Darlene and Henry had not looked at each other even once, both being too involved with the three men who'd broken into their room, but now they did turn to gaze at each other, a quick searching look—will you be any help?—and then faced Mackey again. Her voice lower, less pugnacious, she said, "I already said I'd do it."

Parker said, "What time you supposed to go in there, in the morning?"

"Nine o'clock."

"So we got three and a half hours," he told her, "to figure out what you're gonna do."

Mackey said, "Brenda's never been in jail before. She's never been fingerprinted before, that's why the cops can't get a handle on who she really is. You put an innocent woman in the lockup."

Trying for scorn, not quite making it, Darlene said, "An innocent woman!"

"More innocent than you two," Mackey told her.

"Give them a few minutes," Parker said.

Mackey turned to him. "You mean, leave them alone awhile, let them get dressed, talk it over?"

"That's the best way," Parker said.

Mackey looked around the room. "But what if they decide to use that phone there?"

Parker said, "Then Muriel's got a problem she can't ignore," and the two on the bed gave each other startled looks.

Mackey said, "Yeah, but what if they aren't as smart as they look?"

"No problem," Williams said. He stood, went over to the bed—both people in it flinched, which he didn't seem to notice—and stooped to unplug the phone. "I'll take it with me," he said.

Mackey kept looking around the room. "What if they decide to go out the window?"

Williams, carrying the phone, went to the room's one window. "It's locked," he said. "But it's just the thing you turn, they could unlock it."

A dresser stood between the window and the chair Williams had been sitting in. Parker said, "We'll move the dresser in front of the window. If they move it to get out, we'll hear them from the hall."

Mackey said, "Let me see what's what in the bathroom."

While Mackey went into the adjoining bathroom, Parker and Williams slid the heavy dresser over in front of the window, where it reached halfway up the lower pane. Then Williams stooped to pick up Henry's trousers, go through the pockets, remove the wallet and keys. The couple on the bed watched, tense, together but not together.

Mackey came back to the bedroom and said, "It's okay. No phone in there, and the window's high and small, looks like it's painted shut."

The three moved toward the door, Williams carrying the wallet and the keys and the phone. Parker turned back to say, "You got one chance to get out from under. We'll open the door in fifteen minutes."

6

In the darkness of the hall, with only faint distant streetlight illumination to define the space, Williams put the phone on the floor, and they moved down closer to the living room to have a quiet talk. Mackey said, "What do you think?"

"I think she's smart," Parker said. "She'll figure it out."

"That's the thing," Mackey said. "It's got to come from her."

Williams said, "I think it will."

"If we just scare her," Mackey said, talking out his tension, "and we send her out scared when she talks to the cops, afraid maybe we're back here roasting Henry for lunch, they'll smell it on her. They won't believe the conversation."

Williams said, "It'll be a tough sell anyway."

"She's tough enough to do it," Parker said. "He couldn't do it, but she could."

Mackey said, "But it has to come from her. Her decision, how to make everything okay again."

Williams said, "You gonna stay here while she's doing it?"

Mackey shrugged. "No place else I can think of. And we'll need to keep track of Henry."

"This place could be chancy," Williams said.

Parker said, "I know what you mean. No matter how good she is, they'll think maybe there's something wrong. They'll send somebody here."

"Not with a warrant," Mackey said. "No time, and no excuse."

Parker said, "No, just to eyeball it, while they've still got her there." He nodded toward the front door. "So we'll have to fix that, make it work again. If the beat cop comes around, looks in the windows, tries the doors, everything's okay, then that's it. But if a door's unlocked, that's suspicion, that's probable cause, he'll come right in."

Williams said, "I'm gonna leave it all to you guys. You don't need me any more, and I'm taking Henry's car."

Mackey laughed. "A step up from the Honda."

"This time," Williams said, "I'm getting *out* of this state."

Parker said, "Switch all the cars around. Put ours in the garage, hers outside, then take off with his. That way, in the morning, she drives off, there's no red Saab sitting there that nobody ever saw before."

Williams nodded, grinning. "There's always another detail, huh?"

"Sooner or later," Parker said, "you get to them all."

7

I don't think I can do it," she said.

They were in the kitchen now, seated around the Formica table, because lights at the rear of the house wouldn't draw as much attention. Henry, unshaven, brow creased with worry, wore a pale blue dress shirt, the trousers to a dark blue pinstripe suit, and black oxfords. Darlene was in a high-necked plain white blouse and severe long black skirt; apparently, what she intended to wear to the meeting this morning, a meeting that had now become something else, leaving her uncertain and afraid. She said, "How can I tell them I just changed my mind?"

"People do it all the time," Mackey assured her.

Parker said, "You were hot, you were angry, but now you're cooled off, now you don't want to make trouble for somebody if she really didn't do anything."

"Which she didn't," Mackey said.

"But they're going to look at me," Darlene said.

"They're going to want to know why I changed my mind, and all I'll be able to think about is you two back here, threatening Henry."

Mackey turned to Henry. "Do you feel threatened?"

"Yes," Henry said. He sounded surprised.

Mackey gave him his full attention. "Then let me ask you this," he said. "What do *you* want Darlene to do?"

"I don't want anyone to be hurt," Henry said. "I don't want anybody to be . . . ruined."

"Henry," Mackey said, "you're a braver guy than you know you are. You risk ruin all the time, I know you do, and why? Because you love Darlene. You got your father the jewelry guy to cover for you tonight, because Darlene didn't want to be alone after what happened to her dance studio. That was tough to ask him that, wasn't it?"

Henry nodded. He looked miserable. "Yes," he said.

"I was hysterical," Darlene said. She was apologizing.

"Sure you were," Mackey told her, and said to Henry, "But you did it. You risk everything because you love Darlene, and that's what I'm doing with Brenda. So I'll ask you, what do you want Darlene to do?"

Henry was already shaking his head halfway through the question. "I can't put that on—"

"Yes, you can, Henry," Mackey said. "She's gonna leave here at eight-thirty"—glance at kitchen clock—"less than three hours from now. We're gonna let her walk out the door, get in the car, drive away. Do you want her to go tell the cops she changed her mind, she doesn't think that was Brenda parked there late at night after all, she doesn't want to file a complaint she knows is a lie? Or do you want her to say there's two armed and desperate criminals in her house, and they're holding her lover, you, holding him hostage there? Because then there's a big standoff, a shootout, and a lot of things happen, maybe even the house burns down—"

"The law does that sometimes," Parker said. "They always say it was an accident."

"That's right," Mackey agreed. "Took down a whole neighborhood in Philly a few years ago." To Henry he said, "So all kinds of things could happen, if Darlene tells the law we're in here, and you're in here with us, but the one thing that will *definitely* happen is that you'll be dead. My guarantee, Henry. You won't have to worry about ruin any more."

Darlene, sounding desperate, said, "I *want* to do it, I *know* you two are capable of anything, but I don't know if I *can* do it. I think they'll look at me, and they'll *know*, and then the police will come here and everything will happen just the way you say it will, even though I tried, and we'll *all* be destroyed, every one of us."

Parker said, "The meeting this morning. Is this with the detectives?"

"No, it's an assistant district attorney," Darlene said, "in her office. She's Elise something, I don't remember what."

Parker nodded. "We heard about her," he said. "Let me tell you the exact words we were told about her, by somebody who's seen her and knows her. He said, 'She's a young woman with little experience and no feel for the job.' Is that the way Elise strikes *you*, Darlene?"

Darlene, wide-eyed, said, "How do you people *know* all these things?"

Parker said, "Is that a good description of Elise?"

Darlene thought, then nodded. "Yes. You can tell, she's really mostly bluffing."

"You can outbluff Elise," Parker told her.

Mackey said, "Henry? Do you think she can do it?"

Henry looked at the table, deliberately meeting no one's eye. "Honestly," he said, "I pray she can do it."

Mackey grinned at Darlene. "So it's gonna work out. It isn't gonna be a piece of cake, we all know that, but you can deal with Elise."

"I'll try," Darlene said. She looked at Henry. "I really will do my best."

"I know you will," he said.

Leaning back, a pleased smile on his face, Mackey said, "So now we got plenty of time for a nice breakfast, and we could even rehearse if you want, up to you. I wouldn't want you to be overtrained. And when you leave, your car's in the driveway."

Henry sat up. "You mean, that man took *my* car?"

"He's a local boy," Mackey explained. "He's too well known around here, it seemed a good idea to leave while he could. Don't worry, he'll treat your car well, he won't be going over any speed limits, you can be sure of that. And once Brenda's out of that Fifth Street station, you can call in a stolen car report, no problem. He'll be into some other transportation by then." Getting to his feet, he said, "Darlene, I'm no sexist. Lemme help you make breakfast."

8

At eight-thirty she left, with a rueful look at the ruined front door on the way by. Parker had found hammer and nails in a kitchen drawer, and ripped a piece of jamb from an interior door. With the front door lock in place and the splintered pieces of the old jamb back in position, he'd nailed the new length of wood over the old. From the inside, it looked like hell, but nothing showed on the outside, and the door would lock.

Parker watched her cross to her car, parked now where Henry's had been last night. Her step was firm. She had herself under control.

This was the unknown, starting now. Any time you put somebody on the send, off with the instructions but on their own, you could never be completely certain the glue would hold. She could doublethink herself in the car, on the way to the meeting. She could be blindsided by an unexpected question from somebody there. She could lose her nerve at any step along the way. Or she could hold together and this thing would finally be over.

Darlene got behind the wheel. Carefully she fixed her seat belt. She backed to the street and drove away, not looking toward her house.

Parker turned away from the window. Henry sat slumped on the sofa; he, too, didn't know if she'd hold up. Mackey stood in the doorway, looking at Parker. "Time to make the call?"

He meant to Li. It wouldn't be good to mention that name in front of Henry, just in case things fell apart somewhere down the line. They might still need Li in the near future, and they would need him thinking about them and not thinking about saving his license. Parker said, "Henry, I'll have to lock you in a closet now."

Startled, frightened all over again after a long time of calm, Henry said, "No, you don't! I'll just sit here, I won't make any trouble."

"We have to phone somebody," Parker explained, being slow and patient because it would be better to keep Henry dialed down. "We can't have you listen to it, but I'm not gonna just ask you to wait in the kitchen, right next to that back door."

"It won't be long, Henry," Mackey said, and then he said, "I tell you what. You just go back into the bedroom and close the door. If you open the door, we can see you from here, so don't open the door."

"I won't," Henry promised.

"It'll just be a few minutes, like my friend told you," Mackey assured him. "And then we'll call oley oley in-free, and you come back to the living room. Go now, Henry."

Henry got to his feet. "I won't make any trouble," he said, and went away down the hall.

They watched until the bedroom door closed, and then Mackey said, "I believe him. Henry will not make us trouble."

"Make the call," Parker said.

Mackey went over to sit on the sofa, next to the phone. He pulled Li's card from his shirt pocket and dialed, while Parker stood where he could hear Mackey and watch the hall.

"Mr. Li, please. I'm calling on the Brenda Fawcett matter." Mackey nodded at Parker, and said, "They're patching him through again. I don't think he's ever in his office."

"He doesn't need to be," Parker said.

"No." Mackey looked at Li's card. "He's got all these partners to watch the office." Then, into the phone, he said, "Mr. Li. This is Brenda's friend. No, I know that, you don't have any news yet, but within the hour I think maybe you will. You might even have good news. Yeah, it would be. The thing is, if the news is as good as I think it's gonna be, Brenda's gonna be out from under before we know it. Yeah, that *would* be very nice. Now, if it works out like that, maybe you could give her some change to make a phone call, let me know what's happening. Yeah, I think she should use change to make that phone call. The number's—" and he read off the number from the phone he was using. "I'll be here, hoping for the best. Thank *you*, Mr. Li."

Mackey hung up, and grinned at Parker. "Tell the stud he can come out now," he said.

Parker did, and when Henry got back to the living room he said, "Is it all right if I use the phone?"

Mackey said, "You gotta cover your tracks."

"Muriel believes," Henry said, "I'm spending the night at my father's place. But she'll expect me back some time this morning. So I'll have to call her, tell her I'll stay with my father while they assess the damage at the company, and then I'll have to call my father and say we have to pretend we're still together because I have problems I have to work out even more than before."

Mackey said, "Problems? Doesn't he know what's going on?"

Sheepish, Henry said, "He doesn't know about Darlene. I had to tell him there was somebody I was seeing, which was bad enough, but I said it was somebody he didn't know. He doesn't really like Darlene, and he might not do it if he knew it was her."

"That's a tangled web you're weaving there," Mackey told him, and gestured at the phone. "Go ahead and call. You won't mind if we listen in."

9

At twenty to ten, Mackey was by the living room window, looking out at the street, when he said, "Well, she's telling the story."

Parker, in a chair near the hall, got to his feet. Henry, on the sofa, looked from one to the other, watchful, apprehensive. Looking past Mackey, Parker saw the white sedan just stopping at the curb out front, red block letters RPD on its door. "Rosetown Police Department," he said, and two uniforms came out of the front seat, one on either side.

So Darlene was going through with it. As Mackey had said, she was telling the story, and as they had both known, that meant the law would check her house, just to be sure everything was on the up and up.

As the cops started toward the front porch, Parker said, "Up, Henry."

Rising, Henry said, "Where are we going?"

"Bathroom," Parker told him, as Mackey passed them and went down the hall. "Just till they leave."

Parker shooed him, and Henry followed Mackey, Parker coming third. They went into the bedroom and Mackey said, "Go on in, Henry, we'll be along."

Henry was no trouble. He was like a horse who's learned that obedience is followed by sugar lumps; he went on into the bathroom while Parker and Mackey dragged the dresser away from the window, back to its original position. Then they followed Henry into the bathroom, leaving the door open.

This was the one room in the house that couldn't be looked into from outside. The only window was high and small, its lower half of frosted glass. It was a fairly small room, and they had to stand close to one another, as though in an elevator. Henry stood with his arms folded across his chest. He looked at the wall, and took short audible breaths through his nose.

After a minute, Mackey said, "Henry, take some deep breaths. You're gonna make yourself pass out, you breathe like that."

"Sorry," Henry said. He swallowed and said, "Could I get myself a glass of water?"

"After they leave," Parker said, and from the front of the house came the two-tone call of the doorbell.

They became very silent, even Henry, and after a minute the bell rang again. Another silence, and the rattle of the doorknob, testing the lock.

Quietly, Mackey said, "Now they split, one down either side of the house, look in the windows. Meet at the back, try the door. Go back to the car, call in: Nobody home, no sign of a problem."

The wait seemed long, but probably wasn't, and then they heard another doorknob being tested, at the rear of the house. They'd be looking into the kitchen now, which had been made neat, no evidence left of even one breakfast, let alone four.

Whispering, Henry said, "Do you think they're gone?"

"Let's give them another minute," Mackey said.

They waited another minute, and then Mackey stepped slowly through the doorway, looking to his right, where the bedroom window was. "Looks good," he said, and went on across the bedroom to the hall.

"You can have your water now," Parker said, and Henry drank a glass of water, spilling a little. Then Parker followed him out the door.

No one was looking into the window. They walked down the hall and when they got to the living room and looked out, being careful to stay deep in the room, not too close to the glass, the white RFD car was still there, both cops now inside it. The one in the passenger seat was on the radio.

Henry said, "What are they doing?"

Mackey told him, "The case is in the city. These guys report to their station, their station passes the word to the DA's office in the city, these guys wait here until the word comes back, okay, you're done. Another minute or two. We'll all sit down, and the next time we stand up, they'll be gone."

They were.

10

At twenty-five minutes after eleven, the phone rang. Parker said, "Henry, bedroom. Door closed."

"Go with him," Mackey said, and the phone rang again. "We moved the dresser."

Which meant Henry might be able to get out the window. "Right," Parker said, and followed Henry down the hall. In the bedroom, he said, "Sit around on the other side of the bed," farther away from the doorway. Then he left the door partway open and leaned against the jamb, so he could look at the window and still hear the living room.

If this was Brenda, then they were probably in endgame. If it was some friend of Darlene's, or anybody else, Mackey would say, "Wrong number," hang up, and not answer when they called back. Darlene's answering machine could handle it.

Parker could hear Mackey's voice, but not make out the words. It didn't seem to him that Mackey was talking to Brenda, it didn't have that style to it, but he was having a conversation, not cutting it short, so what was this?

Li. It had to be. Another delay? Another kind of trouble?

Mackey appeared at the end of the hall. "Okay," he said, and walked back into the living room.

"Come on, Henry."

They went back to the living room and Mackey said, "They're stonewalling."

"That was who you talked to before."

"Sure. Darlene's in with this ADA, it's going on and on, and nothing's happening. It should be *over* by now."

"They're trying to break her down," Parker said. "Get her to switch the story back again."

"She won't," Henry said. "If they put pressure on Darlene, I *know* her, she'll just get more and more determined."

"That's good to hear," Mackey said. To Parker he said, "The thing is, before, I only told him there should be news, I didn't say what the news was, and now everything's on hold, so he wants to know what's happening. She's in there, and her lawyer is in there with her, and he needs information." He frowned at Henry and said, "Speaking of which, how much of this is Henry supposed to hear?"

Henry said, "Oh, come on. I'm not stupid. I'm afraid of you two, but that doesn't mean I'm stupid.

Who could you be talking to, this time or last time, except your friend's lawyer? Can I *prove* that? No. Do I hope nobody ever has any reason to ask me what I was doing today? Yes."

"Well, what the hell," Mackey said. "Sit down, Henry, we got a little longer to wait."

Henry sat on the sofa, and Mackey said to Parker, "So he needed to know what was happening, because nothing's coming out of the ADA's office, and I told him, the story is, she flipped, won't sign a complaint, won't identify Brenda. So he's mad, he says once she's flipped it over, they gotta let Darlene go, they gotta let Brenda go, they gotta take a time-out break with coffee and danish. So what he's going to do, he's going to the judge, talk to the judge in chambers, say what's with the delay with this witness, I need to know what's going on here. He'll try to get the judge to raise the question to find out what's going on with the alleged witness, and of course once he does find out the cat's out of the bag and Brenda's out of the Fifth Street station. The judge is not gonna let them browbeat Darlene forever just because she flipped." Mackey shrugged. "Anyway, that's the theory," he said. "I mean, some time today they're gonna have to give up, we know that. It's just we'd rather it was sooner."

"Poor Darlene," Henry said.

Mackey looked at him. "Brenda isn't having that good a day, either, pal," he said.

11

This was a variant on the Stockholm Syndrome. They hadn't planned to hold Henry captive, hadn't planned an encounter with Henry at all. But here he was, and once he was here he couldn't be permitted to just wander off. And his presence would put extra pressure on Darlene to do things right, and not have some sort of mess break out at home.

So they had to spend time together, some hours together, not knowing when or how it would end. Parker kept aloof, but didn't do anything to increase Henry's nervousness; he was tame, let him alone. Mackey was aggressively chummy with him, because that was Mackey's style, to be a pal with a hint of threat inside there. And Henry played his Stockholm part, too, which was to befriend his captors as much as possible, keep them feeling relaxed about him, prove himself useful when and where he could.

Like lunch. At twelve-thirty, still no phone call from

Brenda, no follow-up from Li, Henry broke a long silence to say, "I know this house, I could— If you want,
I could make sandwiches. Darlene usually has cold
cuts, cheese, things like that."

"That's a very good suggestion, Henry," Mackey
said. "We all want to keep our strength up, and you
want to keep yourself occupied."

So all three transferred to the kitchen, where Parker
and Mackey sat at the table while Henry made sandwiches and a pot of coffee. Henry hesitated for a second before sitting with them, then went ahead,
pretending he felt natural about it, and Mackey
grinned at him, saying, "You make a good sandwich,
Henry."

"Thank you."

"I'm not so sure about this coffee, though."

Apologetic, Henry said, "Darlene and I like it
strong. It's espresso mix."

"Huh. I thought I liked it strong, too." He sipped,
thought about it, said, "Okay, maybe." Turning to
Parker, he said, "What do you think of it?"

"It's good coffee," Parker said.

"Okay, then." Mackey grinned some more at Henry.
"It's good coffee," he told him, and they finished their
lunch in silence.

It was while Henry was doing the cleanup that the
phone rang again. Parker said, "Henry, turn off the
water," as Mackey moved to the kitchen wall-phone.

Henry turned off the water and faced the room, back against the sink, hands folded at his crotch.

Mackey got to the phone as it started its second ring: "Yeah?" A big smile creased his face, this one without the usual hint of menace. "So *there* you are! Where are you? He got nice offices? Yeah, I thought he would. You're not calling from his phone, are you? Across the street, outdoors, that's even better. So you're loose now?" Mackey was looking at the clock on the wall, which read almost one-thirty. He said, "So what I think you oughta do, you oughta go back to the hotel and check out, maybe check out at two-thirty, and take a cab to the airport. Okay? Check out at two-thirty, and take a cab to the airport. See you soon, baby." He hung up, and said to Parker, "Li finally levered her out of there."

"They'll tail her," Parker said.

"Oh, sure," Mackey agreed. He didn't seem troubled. Turning to Henry, he said, "Henry, would Darlene have a local map here?"

"I'm not sure," Henry said, with an uncertain look at the kitchen. "I'm not usually here, we have another—"

"Oh, the place at the dance studio!" Mackey said. "Very nice apartment, we saw that."

Henry surprised everybody, including himself, by blushing. As he touched shaky fingertips to his cheek, he said, "I'll see if she has maps here." And did a lot of bustling through kitchen drawers until he got over his embarrassment.

And he did finally come up with a city map, that included downtown, where Brenda was, and Rosetown, the suburb where they were right now, and the airport, west of the city, not far from Stoneveldt. Parker and Mackey sat at the table to study the map while Henry finished at the sink. They didn't speak, but pointed out to each other Brenda's route and their own. As they were folding the map again, the phone rang. Looking at it, on the wall, Mackey said, "No. We don't expect any more calls. Henry, where's the answering machine?"

"In the bedroom."

Parker stood, saying, "Come along."

Henry obediently followed, and the three moved into the bedroom, as the phone continued to ring. They stood in the bedroom, looking at the answering machine on the bedside table, and it clicked, and they moved closer during Darlene's outgoing message. It ended, there was another click, and they listened to Darlene again; much more frantic than on the recording: "Is anybody there? Oh, God, somebody be there!"

Parker reached for him, but before he could grab him Henry had picked up the phone: "Hi, Darlene."

"Henry!" They all heard her because, since Henry hadn't pressed the stop button, the machine was still recording the conversation. "Are you all right?"

"Yes, sure, everything's fine. Are you coming home now?"

"Have they gone?"

"Shit," Mackey said.

Parker said, fast, into Henry's ear, "I'm alone, come home."

"I'm all alone here, Darlene," Henry said. "Everything's fine. Why don't you come home? We don't want to discuss this on the phone."

"Just so they're gone, that's all I ask."

It was hopeless. Parker said, "End it, Henry."

"I have to hang up now," Henry said. "Hurry home, Darlene." And he hung up. Turning away from the phone, he said, "I did my best."

"We know," Parker said.

12

Mackey said, "Henry, wherever she made that call from, somebody was listening."

Henry shook his head. He was ready to apologize for her: "She's not used to this—"

"No time, Henry," Mackey told him. "Cops are on their way *now*. We don't want to talk to them, and neither do you. Go out that front door, walk do not run to the nearest store, call a cab, go home. Goodbye, Henry."

Henry blinked at them both. Parker said, "Now, Henry."

They followed him through the house to the front door. Henry opened it, paused, and Mackey said, "No goodbyes. *Go*."

Henry left. They watched through the front window as he strode briskly to the sidewalk and turned left. Their problem was, they couldn't leave until he was away from here because they didn't want him to know what they were driving. In case he didn't evade the law himself, he shouldn't know that.

Watching Henry's arms swing as he marched away, Mackey said, "The simplest thing, of course, is a bullet in the head. But you know, it's hard to go with the bullet in the head once a guy's made you lunch."

"We can go," Parker said.

They left the house, pulling the breached door shut behind them, and crossed the porch, headed for the garage. "They become real," Mackey explained.

Williams had turned the Saab around before he put it away, backing it into the garage, so they could leave fast if they needed to. They needed to. As Mackey slid behind the wheel, Parker got into the small backseat and curled down sideways to be out of sight, so nobody would have two males in a car with out-of-state plates to think about.

Three blocks later, that turned out to have been a good idea, because four police cars, two of them from Rosetown and two from the city, went tearing by, toward Darlene's house, Tootsie Roll lights flashing on their roofs. As he watched them recede in the rearview mirror, Mackey said, "They're not using their sirens."

Parker sat up and looked out the back window. "Sneaking up on us," he said.

13

The only sensible way to drive from the Park Regal, the hotel Brenda was checking out of, to the airport was to cut across downtown to a highway called the Harrick Freeway. It was more complicated to get to the Harrick from Rosetown, but Parker, in the backseat, gave directions from Darlene's map, and a little after two Mackey took an on-ramp and joined the traffic headed west. Twenty minutes later they saw the exit sign for McCaughey International and took it, Mackey saying, "What we need now is a place we can wait."

That turned out not to be a problem. The four blocks of city street between the freeway and the airport entrance were lined with motels. Mackey pulled in at one in the second block, where the parking area for the attached restaurant was in front, just off the street. Parked to face the traffic, he said, "Now we wait."

"I should do the driving, this part," Parker told him.

"When we get there, you follow Brenda in, I stay with the car. The cops here would make me right away."

"Fine," Mackey said. "Circle the airport and come back for me. Either I'll shake her loose, or I'll see what plane she takes."

They switched places, Parker at the wheel and Mackey beside him, and watched the traffic, which seemed to be about half cabs. They waited a quarter of an hour, and then Mackey said, "There she is," and they watched Brenda go by in the backseat of a taxi, sitting forward, looking in a hurry to be somewhere else.

"There's her tail," Parker said.

"And there's her other one. They put two on her."

The unmarked police car is unmarked, but it's still a police car, still with police equipment, built to government specifications. They're always large American sedans, heavy, four-door, in the lower price range, Plymouths or Chevrolets. They're usually painted some drab color that civilians would never choose but that's supposed to make them less noticeable, and they have the same tires municipalities buy for all their official vehicles, making them the only apparently civilian cars on the road without a white stripe on the tires.

Now, when Parker pulled out from the motel parking lot to follow the followers, both cars were Plymouths, one a dull green, the other a dull tan. Two bulky men rode in the front seat of each. He couldn't see Brenda's cab, but that was all right; the cops could.

They all drove to the airport entrance and in, taking the loop past the terminal buildings. Ahead, first one unmarked car and then the other flashed right-turn signals, so Brenda was going to the terminal for Great Lakes Air, a regional carrier. Parker also pulled over, behind everybody else, stopping just long enough for Mackey to hop out, then angling back into the traffic. One cop was getting out of each car to follow Brenda, the other staying at the wheel. Mackey trailed them all.

This road would eventually circle back to the entrance, where he could swing back to go past Great Lakes Air again. If Mackey was there, he'd stop.

He was taking the left ramp that would lead him around and into the airport again when he glanced in the mirror and saw the green Plymouth behind him. The cop had been hiding in the traffic, but no one else was taking the turn to go back into the airport, so there he was. He'd made a very quick and sure ID as Parker had driven by him. Parker couldn't see him well enough, inside the car back there, but he knew the guy would be on his radio.

This little red car was too identifiable. He couldn't stay in it, but how could he get clear of it without the cop being all over him?

He completed the left-turn U, and this time he noticed the additional lanes that went off to the right, before the terminals, with a big sign above: CARGO.

Those lanes were empty. Parker accelerated into them, widening the distance from the pursuer, the

Saab giving him just that much more juice than the Plymouth could deliver. But he wouldn't have the advantage for long.

This road curved rightward away from the passenger terminals and soon had large storage buildings on its left side, each with an airline name prominent on it. On the right were a high chain-link fence and scrubby fields. A few trucks moved along this road, and Parker snaked through them, looking for an out.

There. On the left, a building with a large open hangar-type entrance on the front. Parker hit the brakes, spun the wheel, hit the accelerator, and roared into the building.

There were trucks in here, too, being loaded or unloaded, with one narrow lane among them and stacks of goods piled high on both sides. Too many workmen moved among the trucks; Parker held down the horn, accelerated, saw the broad open door at the far end, cluttered with electric carts for carrying cargo out to the planes, and braced his forearms on the steering wheel as he slammed down onto the brake, then pushed open his door and slid out of the Saab as it continued to travel at ten miles an hour, straight toward that far opening.

Parker hit the floor rolling, under a truck and out the other side, coming to his feet with the Terrier in his hand. He ran to the front of the truck, saw that the Saab had stopped when it ran into the carts just outside the building, and the Plymouth was just braking to a stop behind it. He ran toward the Plymouth, and its door opened, and the cop got out, and was Turley.

The CID man from Stoneveldt, student of game theory. Of course the law would have him part of this detail, since he knew Parker, had sat across a desk from him twice, told him nobody had ever escaped from Stoneveldt. A small bulky red-haired middleweight, now reaching inside his windbreaker as he slammed the Plymouth's door and took a step toward the Saab.

"Turley!" Parker yelled.

Turley spun around, astonished, and Parker took a flat stance, the Terrier held out in front of himself with both hands. "Hands where I can see them!"

Turley stared all around, not sure what to do. His hand was still inside the windbreaker, but he had to know what would happen if it came out full. Half a dozen workmen, wide-eyed, backed away.

Parker yelled, "I'm a police officer! This man is under arrest!"

"For Christ's sake!" Turley yelled. Now his hand did come out from inside his windbreaker, empty, so he could wave his arms in outrage. "*I'm* the cop!" he yelled. "This man's an escaped—"

Parker had reached him now. "Stop yelling," he said.

Turley blinked at him, trying to catch up.

Parker shook his head. "Game theory," he said. "Chapter two."

"You'll never get out of the airport," Turley told him. "Do you want to add murder one?"

"So everything's going your way," Parker agreed. "So all you have to be is calm, am I right?"

Turley nodded, thinking about that. He'd come down from his rage as quickly as he'd gone up. "You're right," he said. "So why don't you just hand me the weapon and let's let these people go back to work."

"We're getting in your car," Parker told him. "You're driving. If you don't like that idea, I'll give you some murder one and do my own driving."

"You would, too," Turley said. "You proved that with Jelinek."

Parker waited for Turley to get used to the idea. Turley thought for a second, glancing toward the useless workmen, and then shrugged. "You're the escape artist. I'll enjoy watching you at work."

"That's the way," Parker said. Backing away from Turley, he said, "We open our doors at the same time. We get in at the same time."

Turley nodded, and stood with his left hand on top of the car while Parker moved around it to the passenger side and said, "Now."

They opened both doors, slid in, and Parker said, "Don't drive backwards. You can get around the Saab."

Turley put the Plymouth in gear and drove them out of there, through the tight fit between the Saab and a couple of the electric carts, out to the business side of the airport, while behind them the workmen clustered into groups to try to decide what they'd just been witnesses to.

Now they were among the taxiways, with planes landing and taking off some distance away. Clear routes were marked in white paint on the gray concrete, and various vehicles traveled around back here, all staying within the lines.

Turley said, "Do you have some sort of plan in mind?" As though the idea were ridiculous.

To the left were the main terminal buildings. To the right the buildings grew fewer, and some chain-link fence could be seen. Whatever was happening with Mackey and Brenda, there was no point in Parker trying to link up with them again. "To the right," he said.

Turley nodded, and they drove along the rear of the cargo buildings, hundreds of workmen moving around, dozens of vehicles of all kinds, nobody paying them any attention in their unmarked car.

Parker said, "Call in."

Turley seemed surprised. "What do I say, I'm bringing you in?"

"You followed me into that cargo building, I abandoned the red car. You've got the car, but you don't have me. You figure I'm hiding in that building somewhere."

"And I'm standing by?"

"That's right," Parker said. "Waiting for backup."

Turley snorted. "That'll buy you maybe thirty seconds," he said.

"Just do it."

Turley did it, saying it the way Parker had told him to, adding nothing, the dispatcher brisk, in a hurry.

Putting the microphone back on its hook, Turley said, "I'll look like a real idiot, once I finally do bring you in."

Parker said, "I didn't take your gun."

Turley looked at him sideways, looked at the road ahead. "Meaning what?"

"I'm not out to make you feel bad about yourself," Parker told him. "It's just that it's time for me to get to some other part of the world."

"And you figure," Turley said, "if I'm your chauffeur, but you don't disarm me, I didn't lose my weapon to you, that way I've still got my dignity."

"Up to you," Parker said.

"And I'll be easier to control," Turley said, "if I've still got my dignity."

"Up to you."

Turley laughed, not as though he meant it, and said, "Here I was telling you all about game theory. We could have had some nice discussions, back in Stoneveldt."

"I don't think so," Parker said.

"I knew you had something in mind, back there," Turley told him. "I had my eye on you, just not enough."

"I felt the eye," Parker assured him.

"I hope so," Turley said. "There's a gate up there."

Ahead, there was an open guarded gate where the delivery trucks drove in. Four rent-a-cops were on duty there. "Flash the badge," Parker said.

"Naturally."

A gasoline truck was just pulling out when they arrived. Turley lowered his window, dangled the leather folder that held his badge, and Parker put his other arm over the Terrier in his lap as the rent-a-cop leaned down to say, "Help you guys?" He was in his fifties, surely a retired cop himself.

"Undercover work," Turley told him. "Baggage thefts."

The rent-a-cop gave an angry laugh. "We can slow em down," he said, "but nothing will ever stop em." He stepped back and waved them through.

A two-lane road ran along the chain-link fence outside the airport property. Closing his window, Turley said, "Which way?"

"Left." Which would be away from the main bulk of the airport.

This was the flattest part of this flat state, where they'd chosen to put the airport. Miles away to the right, as they rode along beside the fence, Parker could see Stoneveldt looming. So could Turley. He said, "Want me to drop you off there?"

"I don't think so."

The radio squawked. Turley looked at it, looked at Parker. "They're calling me," he said.

"Don't answer."

"I don't have anything cute to say, throw them off the scent?"

"There's nothing cute," Parker told him. "There's just me, going away from here."

The radio squawked again, and Parker said, "Shut it off. There's nothing we need to hear."

Turley switched the radio off, stopping the voice in

midsquawk. They drove a minute in silence, and then Turley said, "I'm state, as I guess you know, but this is a local car we're in."

"Working together to get the bad guys," Parker suggested.

"That's right," Turley said. He seemed serious about it. He said, "A couple years ago, the city police union put a proposal on the table, to city government, install locators in all the cars. You know, bounce off the satellite, tells you exactly where you are, also tells the dispatchers at headquarters exactly where you are."

Parker said, "The politicians didn't want to spend the money."

"You know *that's* true," Turley said. "They said, you boys are local law enforcement, you *know* exactly where you are."

"If they'd spent the money," Parker said, "I'd have to do something else now."

"If they'd spent the money," Turley corrected him, "*and* if I told you about it."

"You'd tell me," Parker said. "You don't want me surprised."

"Well, you're right about that, too," Turley agreed. "We're coming to an intersection up here, which way you want to go?"

Stoneveldt was to the right. "Left," Parker said.

14

It was almost three o'clock. He was out of that city at last, away from the airport and the gathering cops, but he wasn't finished. He couldn't stay in this car much longer, because they'd be putting planes up soon, to look for him. There were two hours of daylight left, far too much, and they were running southwestward away from the city over this tabletop.

Parker said, "What's out in front of us?"

"Corn," Turley said, but then corrected himself. "Not this time of year. Farms, a few little towns, railroad towns."

Railroad towns sounded good. Wouldn't the rails run east-west? "Take your next left," Parker said, which would send them more southerly, to cross a railroad line eventually. Sooner, rather than later.

An intersection grew ahead of them, a gas station and convenience store on one corner, farm equipment dealer diagonally across, nothing on the other two corners but breezy fields with billboards. The intersection was marked by a yellow blinker; Turley waited for a pickup to go by, then turned left. There was little traffic out here.

They rolled along for a while and then Turley said, "Where's Williams?"

"Long gone," Parker said.

Turley nodded. "Dead?"

"No, just gone. Some other state."

"You two didn't stick together?"

"We had different things to do."

"You were both in the jewelry heist, weren't you?"

Parker said, "You hearing my confession?"

Turley chuckled and shook his head. "I'm just interested," he said. "You know, I knew you wouldn't work inside the system, so you didn't surprise me. It's Marcantoni I underestimated."

Just as Parker had known what Turley was doing underneath his words back in Stoneveldt, he understood now what this cosy chat was all about. Turley was a good cop, but he was also mortal. His second job, if he could do it, was to bring Parker in, but his first job was to keep himself alive. Talk with a man, exchange confidences with him, he's less likely to pull the trigger if and when the time comes. Like Mackey deciding to do it the more difficult way because Henry had made him lunch.

That was all right. Part of Parker's job right now was to keep Turley calm, and so long as Turley devoted his mind to his little strategies he would remain calm. So Parker said, "Underestimated Marcantoni? How?"

"I didn't think he'd team with a black," Turley said. "I could see the three of you working something or other, but I thought it'd go a different way."

"That was the way we had," Parker said.

Turley thought about that. "You mean, your original bunch was broken up. You needed to work with the population around you, and most of that, as you know, is pretty sorry stuff."

"That's what you get in there," Parker said.

Turley nodded, agreeing with him. "So you did a little talent search," he said, "came up with the best team, didn't care about any other qualifications."

"Nothing else to care about," Parker said.

"Is that right? Walheim didn't make it, you know."

The abrupt change of subject left Parker blank for a second, and then he remembered. Walheim had had a heart attack. He said, "So he escaped, too."

"You could look at it that way."

They drove in silence a minute, and then Turley said, "You didn't ask me about Bruhl."

"Ask you what about Bruhl?"

Turley looked at him, then faced the road again. "I guess you don't care, but I'll tell you anyway. Bruhl will live and do time. More than Armiston, and in a harder place."

Parker said, "Armiston was dealing with you before you ever talked with me."

"Well, around that time," Turley agreed.

Far away, miles away, a few low buildings were clustered around the road. At the moment, there was no nearby traffic. Parker said, "Pull off the road and stop."

Turley did, and said, "Engine on or off?"

"On. In Park."

Turley did that, and faced Parker. "What now?"

"You know the easy way to take a piece out of its holster," Parker said. "Thumb and forefinger, just holding the butt."

Affecting surprise, Turley said, "I thought you weren't going to take my weapon. I'm keeping my dignity that way."

"You'll get it right back," Parker assured him. "I just don't want you shooting out my tires."

"Oh, I see, we're saying so long now." Turley shrugged. "Okay, fine, here it comes, gentle and easy."

Holding the windbreaker open with his left hand, he grasped his revolver, a .38 Colt Trooper, by the bottom of the butt between thumb and forefinger and slowly lifted it out of the holster strapped around his underarm. Once it was clear, Parker took it away and said, "You got one in an ankle holster?"

"I'm not that kind of cop."

"Show anyway."

Turley lifted both legs of his tan chinos. Black socks above black oxfords, nothing else.

Parker said, "Fine. Now you step out."

"See you again," Turley said.

"I don't think so."

Turley opened his door and climbed out. On the gravel, he leaned to look back in and say, "Kasper, do us all a favor. When they come get you, don't do anything crazy."

"I'll try," Parker said.

Turley nodded and shut the door, as Parker slid over to get behind the wheel. He drove away from there, and a football field's length down the road pulled over again. Triggering the passenger window open, he hurled the Trooper into the field, seeing in that outside mirror Turley, way back there, trudge this way. Parker drove on, mashing the accelerator, holding the Plymouth on this straight flat road above eighty.

The cluster of buildings still looked a long way away.

15

It wasn't a railroad town, one of the freight depots that feed the midwest and help the midwest feed the world. It was a river town, from an earlier era, when barges kept the commerce moving. It was partly kept alive now by the east-west interstate highway that had been built just to its south. Even coming into the town from the north, Parker could see the fifty-foot-high signs of the two competing gas stations at the interstate exit.

Trucks were as good as trains, if you needed to travel fast and not be noticed. The problem now was time; there was no way to go around the town, so Parker had to go through it, all seven of the traffic lights on its main street, past the county courthouse, past the police station and the firehouse, past all the places where his own picture would have been posted now for a week, in a car that half the state was looking for.

He was prepared to cut and run at any second, and

would rely on the weight of the Plymouth, a fully equipped police car under its mufti, to get him through or out of any problem. But nothing happened. Three-fifteen on a midday afternoon, very little traffic in the town, not a local cop in sight. The last traffic light turned green, the city street became a road again, and there was the interstate overpass just ahead, earringed with on-ramps.

Driving under the interstate, he looked at the long sloping shelves of rock to both sides, angled up to meet the bottom of the highway angling down. He could put the Plymouth off the road here, as far up the slope as he could go before the highway would be low enough to hit its roof, and not be seen at all from the air.

But for anybody driving by—particularly any cop—it would be an anomaly. Even if the cop didn't recognize the vehicle or the license plate, he'd wonder why it was there. Parker drove on, out the other side to clear November afternoon sky, and entered the gas station on his right, where a second big sign, aimed at the traffic on the highway, blared EASY ON EASY OFF.

This was much more than a gas station. There was a café attached, and a convenience store. For the long-haul truckers, or anyone else who wanted, showers and cots were available.

There were two parking areas, separating trucks from cars, and the truck area was more full. Parker drove in among the cars and parked as much in the center of the pack as possible. Before he left the Plymouth, he searched its glove compartment and trunk, finding a shotgun, a Colt automatic, flares, a first-aid kit, handcuffs, a box of Ace bandages, an extra radio. He left it all, with the key in the ignition, and walked away toward the convenience store.

Money could start to be a problem. He had a few hundred dollars on him, but no credit cards, no way to get quick cash except a minor-league holdup that would bring more trouble than profit. Claire's two thousand through Brenda hadn't gotten to him, and wouldn't. He had no choice but to just keep moving, as fast as possible.

In the convenience store, he bought half a dozen small cans of tomato juice and a box of crackers. Leaving the store, stowing the food inside his jacket, he turned toward the truck parking area but then veered away again. They had a guard on it.

A lot of these places had trouble with minor thefts out of the trucks while the truckers ate or slept or showered. Or screwed. So the gas station would hire a guard, just a big dumb guy with a billy club to walk around among the trucks, keep them safe. He was always a guy guaranteed to be bored enough to welcome the rare opportunity to use the club; though he might ask one or two questions while reaching for it.

Parker had meant to get inside a truck that looked to be headed eastbound, but not if it meant leaving a dead guard outside. So he turned away and walked over to one of the concrete picnic tables nobody ever uses, and waited.

He knew what he was waiting for. A couple, in their forties or fifties. More and more, the owner-driven big rigs are operated by couples, people whose kids are grown or who never happened to have any. Wife and husband share the driving and take turns sleeping in the cot behind the main bench seat. They own the truck together, so nobody's an employee. It keeps her out of the house and him out of trouble, and it works out better than two guys going into a partnership.

He wanted a couple because he needed to be invited aboard. A singleton trucker might not like the look of Parker as a passenger, might be more curious about him than helpful toward him. A male pair wouldn't want another male in their midst. But for a husband-wife, with nothing but each other and the radio for all those miles and all those days, it would be like inviting somebody onto their porch. A little conversation, a little change of pace.

He waited twenty minutes, watching people go by, getting a few inquisitive stares. He drank one of the cans of tomato juice and went over to toss the can in the trash basket, then went back to sit and wait some more.

Then here they came. He knew they were right the instant they walked out of the café. Midfifties, both overweight from sitting in the truck all the time, dressed alike in boots and jeans and windbreakers and black cowboy hats, they were obviously comfortable together, happy, telling each other stories. Parker rose and walked toward them, and they stopped, grinning at him, as though they'd expected him.

They had. "I knew it," the man said, and said to his wife, "Didn't I tell you?"

"Well, it was pretty obvious," she said.

Parker said, "You know I want a lift."

The man gestured at the building behind him. "We saw you sitting out here, speculated about you."

The woman said, "We don't have that much to distract us."

"You were here too long to be waiting for a partner," the man said. "Or a wife. So you want a lift. But you let half a dozen fellas go by. I said to Gail here, 'He's looking for a couple, cause he knows we won't turn him down.' "

"After I saw you throw the tomato can away," she said, "and not litter, I said, 'All right. If he asks, we'll say yes.' "

"If you're headed east," the man said.

"I am," Parker said, and put his hand out. "My name's John."

"I'm Marty," the man said, "and this is Gail."

They started walking, Parker beside them, and Marty said, "Where you headed?"

"New Jersey."

"Well, we'll get you to Baltimore, and you can work it out from there."

"I could *walk* it from Baltimore," Parker said.

16

Their truck was a blue Sterling Aero Bullet Plus, one of the biggest long-haul tractors on the road, with room enough to stand upright in the sleeper box behind the seat, and a separate door to that area on the right side, behind the regular passenger door. No one would be using the bunk right now; Gail would drive, with Marty in the middle on the wide bench seat, and Parker on the right.

"We're still on California time," Marty said, as Gail started them up, "which is why the late lunch. We probably won't want dinner until late, either."

"That's fine," Parker said.

The truck nosed out of its place, Gail turning the big wheel, and as they followed the truck lane around behind the station building, headed for the interstate on-ramp, Parker saw a state police car moving slowly along an aisle over in the other parking area, the one for cars. He didn't turn his head to watch it, and neither Marty nor Gail seemed to notice it.

It was a different experience, being up here in this high cab, streaming straight eastward toward the night, the remnants of red sun low to the horizon behind streaks of cloud and pollution. You looked down on the tops of cars, across at other truckers, and it felt as though the load in the trailer was pushing the cab rather than the cab providing the power. Gail set the cruise control button on the steering wheel to 77, and they ran smoothly in the river of moderate traffic.

Once they were up to speed, part of the flow, Gail said, "There we are. Anybody want the radio?"

"Not now, Gail," Marty said. "You get tired of local news." To Parker he said, "Don't you?"

"Yes, I do," Parker said.

Marty said, "You don't mind my saying so, you don't seem like a man spends much time in parking lots, looking for a ride home."

"I'm not," Parker said. He'd known he'd have to explain himself, and was ready. Everybody on the highway believes the country-and-western songs, so he'd sing them one. "I'm embarrassed to tell you," he began. "Usually—excuse this, Gail—usually I got good instincts when it comes to women."

"Ho ho," Marty said.

"Well, there I was in Vegas—"

"Ha *ha!*" Marty said.

Gail, looking at him past her husband, said, "I thought they cleaned Vegas up."

"Maybe so," Parker said. "But Vegas cleaned me *out.* I hope you don't mind, I don't want to go through the details—"

"Not at all," Gail said.

"I learned my lesson, this time," Parker assured them. "Back in Jersey, I got a car, and a house, and a bank account, so I'll be okay."

"Good," Gail said.

"Just don't introduce me to anybody between here and there," Parker said. "You know what I mean."

"Hah," Marty said.

Jouncing woke Parker out of therapeutic sleep, and when he lifted his head, oriented himself in the dashboard lights, they were leaving the highway, bouncing down a badly maintained off-ramp toward a small country road. Parker had been sleeping against the right door, and Marty was now at the wheel, Gail nowhere in sight, the curtain closed over the sleeper box. Parker swallowed. "What's up?"

"Oh, could be delays, up ahead," Marty said. "Seemed like a good idea, go around it."

"Go around what?"

"A few fellas coming the other way," Marty explained, "mentioned on the radio, there's a roadblock a few miles up ahead."

"Roadblock?" Parker shifted in the seat, trying to

get more comfortable after sleeping in his clothes. "After drunk drivers?"

"Probably," Marty said. "They always take the opportunity, long as they've got you stopped, check every goddam thing they can think of. Looking for drugs, illegals, overweight. Check your license, your manifest, your log. You can kill an hour, one of those places, just on line, waiting your turn. Better to get off, take one of these slow roads, come back up on the highway a little later."

"Well," Parker said, "drunk drivers can be trouble."

"Sure they can," Marty agreed. "Get em off the road. But it could be anything, up there. Maybe they're looking for somebody escaped from prison, that happens sometimes, I even heard it on the local news, somewhere along here, the trip out."

"They don't stay out long," Parker said.

"You're right." Marty hesitated, wanting to say something, not sure he would, then said, "Let me tell you a little story, long as Gail's asleep back there. And even if she isn't asleep, she can't hear us."

"All right."

"Not that she doesn't *know* the story," Marty went on. "God knows, she does. Anyway, I was dumb like you about a woman once." He nodded his head at the curtain behind them. "Before I met Gail."

The road they were on now was two-lane asphalt with potholes, and the big truck had to slow-dance along it, Marty steering all the time. He said, "But I was even dumber than you, for even longer. Well, I was younger, too. But the fact is, I wound up doing four years—well, almost four years—in a state pen. Attempted robbery. Seven to ten, got out in the minimum."

"Four years is a long minimum," Parker said.

"Oh, you know it." Marty concentrated on the road awhile, then said, "I know there's fellas belong in there, I know there's fellas I'd *prefer* was in there, but after being in there myself I could never put a man in a cage, personally. Never."

"I know the feeling," Parker said.

"If a man wants to learn from his mistakes, fine," Marty said. "You look at me. You see the job I gave myself. Coast-to-coast hauling. You can't get much farther from a four-man cage inside a six-hundred-man cage inside a four-thousand-man cage."

"Not much farther," Parker agreed. He looked out at the road, picked out by the white lights of the truck, with the ghosts passing just outside the light of the occasional farmhouse, gas station, diner, bar, all of them shut and dark. The dashboard clock read 4:27 A.M. He said, "What time zone is this?"

"This," Marty told him. "We change it to keep track. Easier than changing our stomachs."

"There's your roadblock," Parker said. Far off to their left, at a higher elevation, the cluster of red-white-blue shimmering lights was like a jamboree for machinery.

Marty looked over there, then back at the road. "No sense going through that," he said.

Parker said, "Won't they see all the lights on this rig, over here, come over to see who we are?"

"Not if they're looking for a runaway," Marty said. "A runaway won't be driving something like this."

"All right."

"They're not evil geniuses, over there," Marty said. "They're just boys doing their job. Go up on the highway, hassle anybody comes through. So that's what they're doing. Six o'clock, they're told, go on back to the barracks, that's what they'll do. They aren't *hunters*. They're just boys doing a job."

They went through an intersection marked by a yellow blinker, and Marty said, "Another fifteen, twenty miles, there'll be an on-ramp. We'll be fine from there."

17

Claire rolled over when he walked into the room. Her eyes gleamed in the darkness, but she didn't say anything as she watched him move. Out of his pocket and onto the dresser went the three Patek watches that were the only result of the jewel job. He stripped and got into bed and then, folding into his arms, she said, "Gone a long time."

"It felt like a long time."

"I knew you'd be back," she said.

"This time," he said.